The Enemy in the Blanket

BOOKS BY
ANTHONY BURGESS

NOVELS

Eve of St Venus
A Vision of Battlements
Time for a Tiger
The Enemy in the Blanket
Beds in the East
The Right to an Answer
The Doctor is Sick
The Worm and the Ring
Devil of a State
A Clockwork Orange
The Wanting Seed
Honey for the Bears
Nothing like the Sun
Tremor of Intent
Enderby Outside
M.F.

BIOGRAPHY AND LITERARY CRITICISM

The Novel Now
*Here Comes Everybody – An Introduction to James Joyce
for the ordinary reader*
Shakespeare
Urgent Copy

PHILOLOGY

Language Made Plain

* * * * *

(as Joseph Kell)
One Hand Clapping
Inside Mr Enderby

(as John Burgess Wilson)
English Literature – A Survey for Students

ANTHONY BURGESS

The Enemy in the Blanket

HEINEMANN : LONDON

William Heinemann Ltd
15 Queen Street, Mayfair, London WIX 8BE
LONDON   MELBOURNE   TORONTO
JOHANNESBURG   AUCKLAND

First published 1958
Reissued 1968
Reprinted 1972
© by ANTHONY BURGESS 1958

434 09813 2

Printed in Great Britain by
Redwood Press Limited
Trowbridge, Wiltshire

"Their coming and going is sure in the night: in the plains of Asia (saith he), the storks meet on such a set day, he that comes last is torn to pieces, and so they get them gone."

—ROBERT BURTON:

A Digression on the Air

The Malay State of Dahaga and its
towns and inhabitants do not really
exist.

I

The Chinese captain and the Malay second pilot worked stolidly through the check-list.

"Lap-straps, no smoking?"

"*Sudah.*"[1]

"Hydraulic hand-pump?"

"*Tutup.*"[2]

"Carburettor heat?"

"*Sejuk.*"[3]

It was Chinese New Year, the first day of the Year of the Monkey. The passengers had driven through the hot morning town to the airport, slowed or stopped by the Lion-dance swaying through the streets. Young slim-waisted Chinese had crashed gongs, looking somehow Mexican in wide-brimmed straw hats, and the brisk sweating dancer had leapt and run and bowed and advanced and retreated. He had been encased from the shoulders up in the round ugly lion head, while, yards of fluttering cloth away, a small boy had pranced as the tail. Into the open mouth of the Lion people had stuffed, for good luck, little red parcels or *ang pows*. But here, on the brown-grassed airfield, it was just another flying day, nearly time for take-off to the northern fringe of the peninsula.

In Victor Crabbe's mouth a tongue was stuffed like a parcel, a *pow* by no means *ang*. In his head a Lion-dance circled and thumped to loud gong-crashes. Last night he

[1] Done   [2] Shut   [3] Cold

1

had been smothered with Chinese New Year hospitality. Bird's nest, shark's fin, sucking pig, boiled duck, bamboo shoots, bean sprouts, huge staring fish, sweet-and-sour prawns, stuffed gourds, crisp fried rice and chicken-wings. And whisky. Glass after glass of it, neat. *Kung Hee Fatt Choy*. That meant roughly, a Happy New Year. One mustn't lose face; one couldn't say, "No more whisky". He lolled back, eyes closed, ears closed too to his wife's quiet weeping.

Fenella Crabbe sniffed into her handkerchief, and the Sikh traveller in the seat across the aisle smiled with sympathy. It was hard to leave old friends, a loved house, a known town. But duty was duty. Where the British were sent, there they had to go. That was how they had built their Empire, an Empire now crashing about their ears. The Sikh smiled at the vanity of human aspirations. He had been, in his earlier, less prosperous, days, a fortune-teller. He was not that now, he was . . .

Fenella Crabbe read yet again the anonymous letter. It had been delivered into her hands by a small Tamil boy as they stepped into the taxi that morning. It was typed—heavy old office-Oliver type—on greyish paper. The letter ran:

Dear Sister,

My heart has swelled often and again with humble appreciation that you and your husband not like rest of white men in this country. For they suck from bounteous earth like greedy pigs from udder of mother-sow the great riches of rubber which Indians planted in prehistoric ages. Laughing haughtily, they drink at white men's club and spurn their brothers of skin of different hue. But your husband and you, Sister, in no

2

manner like that. For you have freely mingled and show love to your poorer brothers and sisters.

But, O Sister, perhaps you are misguided. Perhaps, in poetic words of base Indian, you love not wisely but too well. And here I refer to your husband the teacher whose brain, though it contain knowledge to bestow in overflowing measure and bounty on eager learning youth, it can yet stoop to base act of sexuality. For it is known that he has for many months sated uncontrolled lust on simple Malay girl who is widow and orphan, both. And she herself believing that the child that is natural consequence shall have white skin and she become object of revilement among her people.

Sister, I tell you in all truth, which is precious jewel, though worn on toad's head. And I say that you warn him to show care in new place whither you go. For there men are men of strong passions and much subject to the green-eyed monster that mocks the meat it feeds on. And they will hit him on the head with little axes and English blood will stain Malayan soil.

Closing now with good wishes and hopes and blessing of our one father God for your new state and much happiness in work and social amenities.

The Voice of the East.

Postscript. You ask others here and they telling you the selfsame story.

"For God's sake, stop crying," said Crabbe.

The number two engine back-fired. Soon there was an all-enclosing vibration, perhaps like the rumble of blood that surrounds the torpid fœtus. The Chinese pilot released the brakes, advanced the throttles.

"And to think this was going on all the time," shouted Fenella, barely audible above the engines. "I thought we had no secrets from each other."

The gongs throbbed through the engines and the Lion jumped and came down with a crash in his brain. "But it finished long ago. There was no point in telling you."

"And she's going to have a baby."

"WHAT?"

"A BABY."

"Well, it won't be mine. I can prove it."

"You're disgusting. I'm going to leave you."

"WHAT?"

"LEAVE YOU."

The Sikh traveller smiled in his beard. They quarrelled among themselves. The beginnings of dissolution. But the future was bright for him, Mohinder Singh. Let them not say that the Sikhs were fit only for the police or the bullock-cart or the hard bed of the night watchman. Let them not say that the Sikhs had no aptitude for business.

Crabbe took a glucose sweet from the air hostess and crunched it irritably. Fool. She needn't have known. But, unthinking, he had said, wearily, that she wasn't a widow but a divorcée and wasn't an orphan but had a very vigorous set of parents and grandparents away in a remote village. And that, of course, had done it. If only he hadn't been feeling crapulous, if only he didn't still feel crapulous. Crabbe looked with favour at the air hostess. Her name, according to the little board by the cockpit door, was Molly de Cruz. Eurasian. Crabbe had a swift cinematic vision of the glory of Malacca and the coming of the urgent Portuguese. She was long-legged, ample under the uniform jacket, a sweep of rich hair under her cap. Now she danced up the aisle with newspapers, hand-

4

ing out *The Timah Gazette* and *The Singapore Bugle,* a Malay journal in proud sweeping Arabic headlines, a cramped sheaf of drilled Chinese ideograms. Crabbe shook his head at her, smiling refusal with what he hoped was debauched charm. Fenella bent angry brows over a front page, taking in nothing of the Singapore riots, the 'Clear Out British' banners above toothy smiles and brown feet, the smirk of a new strip-tease artiste from Hong Kong.

Deep below them was deep jungle and, far to the west, the Malacca Straits. They moved with speed towards the air of a strange land, Negeri Dahaga, Malay country washed by the China Sea, a State of poor honest fishermen and rice-planters. It was a land which had been tardy in yielding to the kindly pressure of the British, and Chinese and Indian traders had been slow to follow the promise of peace and cold justice: Malay land, where the Chinese kept to their shops and ate pork in secret. A mere fifty years before, the Siamese had waived, as also with the neighbour States of Kelantan and Trengganu, the *bunga mas,* the rich golden flower of tribute. A British Adviser had come at a time when a gardened Residency and Sikh guards and a coach-and-four had long been a common-place on the West Coast. And there the Adviser had found, and his successors found still, that the State was only nominally in the hands of a Sultan. Dahaga was ruled feudally by an hereditary officer called the Abang, a man with such titles as Scourge of the Wicked, Friend of the Oppressed, Loved of God, Father of a Thousand, who claimed descent from the fæces of the White Bull of Siva.

Traditionally, even the installation of the Abang was far more magnificent than the Sultan's coronation. Silver trumpets clamoured and drums thumped and Javanese xylophones clattered with an ominous noise of dry bones.

An age-old Hindu prayer was intoned while the Islamic leaders looked placidly on. The names of some of the Abang's ancestors were chanted, great heroes who had tried to subdue the world to the True Faith: Al Iskander the Great, Aristotle, Mansor Shah, Averroes, D'Albuquerque, Abu Bakar and others. The Abang s feet were washed in goat's milk and his testes blessed and anointed behind a gold-thread curtain. Veiled girls danced to the skirl of Indian pipes, rich curries were eaten and mounds. of cold rice distributed to the poor. And the Sultan smiled and fidgeted and was sent away to supervise his four quarrelling wives and play chess with his attendants, seeing himself, crowned but impotent, static or retreating on the chequered board. Meanwhile the Abang ruled, collecting many dues, lounging in limousines, impatient of the gentle restraints of Western law. From the West he desired only cars and fair-haired women.

The chief town, Kenching, was bulbous with mosques and loud with the cries of many muezzins. Islam was powerful. During the fasting month police squads dragged out sinful daytime eaters from house or coffee-shop. Non-attendance at the mosque on Friday—if discovered—was heavily fined. Polygamy was practised and divorcée prostitutes were thick on the evening streets. But ancient Hinduism and primitive magic prevailed in villages and suburbs. The *bomoh*, or magician, cured pox and fever, presided at weddings and grew rich on the fees of fishermen who begged prayers for a good catch. Gods of the sea and gods of the rice-grain were invoked, threatened, rewarded. And from the north came Siamese Buddhism to complicate further the religious patterns of Dahaga.

History? The State had no history. It had not changed in many centuries, not since the Chinese had stepped ashore and soon retreated, carrying its name back in three ideograms: DA HA GA. The British had hardly disturbed the timeless pattern. The rivers were still the main roads, though the railway train puffed in from the south once a week and an aeroplane came daily. There were cinemas and a few hotels, some British commercial firms in poky offices. But Dahaga regarded all these as a rash that might go, leaving the smooth timeless body unchanged. Or the British might be absorbed, as the Siamese had been in the days of the Occupation, when the Japanese had moved west and south, leaving Dahaga to their jackal friends from Thailand. The future would be like the past—shadow-plays about mythical heroes, bull-fights and cock-fights, top-spinning and kite-flying, sympathetic magic, axeing, love-potions, coconuts, rice, the eternal rule of the Abang.

All that Victor Crabbe knew was that he was appointed headmaster to a school where the medium of instruction was English. That such a school should exist at all in Dahaga was probably due to an oversight on the part of some Abang of the past, one who had tasted whisky and become momentarily Anglophile or had grunted in his sleep what sounded like assent to the gentle recommendations of a British Adviser. Victor Crabbe had never been a headmaster before, and it was as much apprehension as crapula that had distracted him into admitting that the anonymous letter-writer had spoken some truth. Otherwise he would have said, "The only thing to do with such letters is to burn them and forget about them." But he had always been convinced that Fenella would find out sooner or later about his liaison with Rahimah. It had never seemed necessary to volunteer the information. He had just felt that, if she found out, she would laugh in her

7

gay sophisticated way and cry, "But, darling, how amusing. What was it like?" And, in a way, he didn't want her to take it so light-heartedly, because Rahimah had meant something to him. So he let things slide. Now here she was, sobbing like any suburban housewife, all jealous woman, eyes red and cheeks swollen, threatening to leave him. However, this too might be part of a New Year hangover. She had washed down the boiled duck with much gin. Best to say nothing and wait.

Crabbe looked at what he could see of the other passengers. A squat Chinese, deep in his newspaper of ideograms. A turbaned *haji* asleep. Two Malay wives, meek behind their husband. Meek perhaps with air-sickness, for Malay women were normally all earth and spirit. A redhaired Englishman with brief-case and dark glasses. A bald Tamil, blue-black above the white shirt. And a smiling Sikh.

The Sikh was smiling with full-bearded compassion at Fenella, who was retching quietly into a paper bag. The intrepid British of the past, who had ruled the waves. Ah, they were becoming an effete race. The least thing upset them now. And the man next to her, her husband, he too had turned green. The white man had turned green. Ah, very good. He, Mohinder Singh, had never felt better.

"I feel so ill," said Fenella, and she flopped back in her seat. Crabbe took her hand and she suffered the pressure of his fingers.

"Never mind, darling."

"How could you?" she whispered, from a lifeless mouth, eyes closed.

"It won't happen again."

Though it probably would, despite the passionate men with axes.

Soon the tawny land of Dahaga began to ogle them and then, brazenly, to raise its arms towards them from its sleepy sandy bed. Its coconut-palms swayed mannequin-like, voluptuous in the sea-wind. They saw the white-washed name on a long attap roof, the whispered introduction rising to a shout: KENCHING.

Molly de Cruz brought round her charger of glucose sweets. LAP-STRAPS. NO SMOKING, said the electric sign. They dropped to earth and the aircraft changed from a flying ship to a great awkward lolloping bus.

Mohinder Singh slowly lost his full bearded smile of confidence. He became agitated. There was something he had to communicate to the memsahib. She had been sick, she still looked green (ha!), but she walked now with grace towards the aircraft's open mouth, towards the huge sun-light and marine sky outside. Mohinder Singh followed the man her husband, struggling with something in the back pocket of his white trousers. At leisure, below, he would, if only he could find the accursed thing.

"They said he'd meet us," said Crabbe. "I can't see a single European waiting anywhere." They walked towards the terminal of two long huts, their luggage trundled after them. Two Malay women in sarongs, white powder, high heels greeted their fellow-wives. Their husband, who carried only a paper carrier, marched off his hens to a waiting car, his belly proud before him. The Chinese passenger was greeted in loud Hokkien by a loose-shirted yellow cadaver, all big teeth and spectacles. The red-haired Englishman shambled off with his brief-case. The Crabbes had much luggage, it had to be passed by the Customs official, they had to wait. But there was definitely no one waiting for them.

"You ought to check on these things," said Fenella.

9

"It was in the letter, in black and white," said Crabbe. "Official."

Mohinder Singh pulled out his wallet and began to search desperately. Identity card. Lottery ticket. A broken comb. A picture of his fat small niece. A soiled paper with Chinese magic numbers. A folded pamphlet about Guru Gobind Singh. Some ten-dollar notes. But not what he was looking for.

On the counter of the stifling Customs shed the Crabbes' luggage was ranged. A Siamese girl in a short-skirted uniform asked them if they had anything to declare. No, they had nothing.

Standing splay-footed at the back of the terminal were Malays of a kind that Crabbe had never seen before. Their legs were bare and muscular, bidding their feet hold down the earth as though, in this place of flying ships, the very sandy soil might take off. On their heads were dish-towels wrapped in loose turban-style, with apices waving in the wind. They wore torn sports-shirts and old sarongs. Their faces were lined and their eyes keen. They were silent. In their hands . . .

Crabbe felt fear tremble through his hangover. No, this was impossible. Damn it all, he'd only just arrived. Had the word been passed already? Had they been told off by her relatives on the West Coast, the message drumming through the thick jungle? In their hands were long cloth bundles, but their fingers clutched a recognisable heft, and Crabbe felt in anticipation the sharp axe-edge pierce his skull or, at best, the thud of the dull heavy blunt back.

"Lady," said Mohinder Singh. "It is misfortune that I mislay my business card. My name is Mohinder Singh. You are coming to Kenching. You will want many things for your fine house. My shop is very new shop on Jalan

Laksamana. Fine silks and curtainings and cloths of all kinds. Bedspreads. Camphor-wood chests. You come and you will be satisfied. For babies all things too."

"Don't mention babies," said Crabbe.

"Look," said Fenella. "They're coming here. For us. They've got weapons."

"Yes," said Crabbe. "They've got weapons."

"This is all your fault," said Fenella, unreasonably. "Messing about with native women."

"Don't retreat," said Crabbe. "Look them in the eye."

The men advanced steadily, five of them, a small boy in the rear, he too with a bundle, learning the trade. The Customs girl paid no attention, chatting to one of the airport underlings. Soon the eldest axe-man, a vigorous patriarch, snarled briefly at the others, who then just stood and stared without rancour at the intended victim. With a relief so immense that it brought the hangover hurtling back, Crabbe saw that their quarry was the shopkeeper Sikh.

"What's he saying?" asked Fenella. The patriarch was using a terse barking language that seemed all vowels and glottal checks. But Crabbe could understand something of this strange dialect, for his Malay tutor in Kuala Hantu had given him an account of its phonology. The senior axe-man approached the cowering Sikh and told him that there was no animosity on the part either of himself or of his colleagues. He was just doing this for a friend. The Sikh well knew that the friend was soon to appear in court on a charge of stealing one tea-towel from the Sikh's shop. It would be a good thing for the Sikh to drop the charge. Indeed, he was now about to be formally warned to drop the charge, for friends must be helped, without friendship the world is nothing. If he would heed this warning he would not thereafter be molested further. All this was told in rapid root-words with little structural linking. Then the warning came.

The axe thudded but dully on the Sikh's mass of turban and unshorn hair. The Sikh sat on the ground and moaned a while. The patriarch took from the waist of his sarong two cigarettes. He told the Sikh that this was the only payment he had taken, as the work was done for a friend. He put one cigarette in his own mouth and handed the other to the Sikh. To show there was no real animosity. A job, as you might say.

"Foolish old man," said one of the axe-gripping juniors. "He is a *Benggali tonchit*. It is against their religion to smoke."

"True," said the patriarch. "The world is full of pork-stuffing infidels. Let us go." And off they went, the small boy waiting respectfully to bring up the rear.

"What a shame," said Fenella to Mohinder Singh. "Are you dreadfully hurt?"

"See," said Mohinder Singh, "my business cards were in my turban. They dislodged with the strike of the weapon. In Dahaga such things happen. Law and order not possible. Please take one card, lady." And he tottered off to the rear of the terminal. Soon he could be seen on a bicycle, twisting drunkenly down the road.

"Now what do we do?" asked Fenella. "We can't stay here all day. I feel terrible. I don't think I'm going to like it here. For God's sake ask somebody something."

Crabbe asked the Customs girl. Did she know where Mr. Talbot lived? She did not. Mr. Talbot was the State Education Officer . She knew of no such appointment. Did she know of a school called the Haji Ali College? She had never heard of it. How far was it from the airport to the town? That she knew: eight milestones. Was it possible to get a taxi? Not from here. Was there a telephone available? There was not.

"Helpful, aren't they?" said Crabbe. The sun had started its afternoon stint, and the sweat welled in his shirt.

"We'll have to go somewhere," said Fenella. "I feel like death. Is there no way we can get into the town?"

"Hitch-hike, that seems to be the only way," said Crabbe. "That looks like the main road. Let's get on to it."

"Oh, what an awful bloody mess," moaned Fenella. "You never could organise anything. Time and time again you let me down."

Crabbe asked the Customs girl and the interested ground-staff of three if they could leave their luggage here at the airport and call for it later. The girl replied that it was not advisable, as there were many thieves. Perhaps, suggested Crabbe, it could be stored in some office that had a lock and key? That was not possible, for there was no such office.

Now at that moment two of the turbaned Malay axe-men reappeared, this time without their axes. They both pedalled decrepit trishaws and one of them called out: "*Taksi, tuan?*"

"Where?" said Fenella with hope. "I can't see any taxi."

"They call these things taxis," said Crabbe. "Come on, better than nothing."

And so the luggage was piled on to one trishaw, and Fenella and Victor Crabbe wedged themselves into the cane seat of the other. They had to sit close, like lovers, and Crabbe even had to put his arm round her back.

"Don't sit so near," she said. "I hate you to touch me."

"Oh, hell," he snapped. "I'll walk if you want me to." He was hating everything and everybody. But he did not move. Soon the sullen journey commenced, hard muscular legs circling, on the sandy road to the town. On their right was the conventional tropical paradise of sea and palms, slim girls bathing in soaked sarongs, attap huts and waving children. On their left were paddy-fields and massive buffaloes. Above them merciless blue and the sun at its zenith.

A few cars passed them, small Austins with huge families crammed inside, the children waving derisively. Once a Cadillac passed, empty but for a proud smoking uniformed chauffeur, bearing as number-plate the legend 'ABANG'.

"Ominous that," said Crabbe. "Tyres, I mean. I wonder how our car will fare on this road. When it gets here."

"If it gets here. I suppose you've messed that arrangement up, too."

"Oh, shut up."

"You shut up. How dare you speak to me like that."

"Oh, shut up."

But then they stopped their wrangling, for ahead of them a car had halted. A dusty car, and from it peered a face, a European face, and then a greeting arm.

"A sort of Livingstone and Stanley," said Crabbe. "Nice of him."

The face was pale, the eyes pale, the hair almost white, the eyebrows invisible, the eyelashes seemingly singed away. It was a young face, however, pointed, pixyish.

"Better if I gave you a lift," said the stranger. "You shouldn't really go around on those things, you know. I mean, white men don't do it, and all the rest of it, not here they don't, and besides there's an Emergency on. Communists leap from the sea, like Proteus. You must be new here. No car?"

"It's coming by train. Look here, I know you. In England somewhere. Or Army?"

"I was Air Force. You a University man? I was at . . ."

"You read Law. I read History. Something-man, something-man . . ."

"Hardman."

"Hardman, by God. Robert Hardman. Well, of all the . . ."

"Rupert Hardman."

"I'm Crabbe."

"Well, good God, who would have thought . . ."

Handshakes, pommellings, cries of incredulity. Patiently Fenella waited. At length she said, "Manners, Victor."

"Victor, of course. And this is Mrs. Crabbe?"

"Sorry. Rupert Hardman, Fenella. And what are you doing here?"

"Law. Still law. You posted here?"

"Education: I should have been met. By Talbot. Do you know the man? We were trying to get into town. I suppose somebody there would . . ."

"Not in town. He lives somewhere near here, I know. Have you much luggage?"

"A few cases. The rest is coming by train. With the car."

"Well, well, incredible. Get in. I'll take you to Talbot's place. Queer sort of chap. Queer sort of set-up. The whole place, I mean. You must come round to the hotel sometime. The Grand, a bit of a misnomer. Talbot's a bit off the beaten track."

They paid off the trishaw men and loaded the luggage into the boot and on to the back seat. Fenella looked curiously at the pale-headed lawyer, the shabby upholstery, the stuffed ashtray which spoke of failure.

"Mortimer's out here, too. You remember him?"

"He was the chap who . . ."

"That's right. He's doing well. Married a Chinese widow. Money in tin."

"And you? Married? Doing well? This is incredible, you know. I mean, meeting like this."

Hardman shrugged his thin shoulders. "I shall be. Both, I think. Fairly soon. That is, if everything goes right. Things don't always go right, you know. Not here."

"I know."

Hardman turned left, entering a lane bumpy with sand-drifts and ruts. The car jolted and bounced and creaked. "Springs not very good, I'm afraid. This gear keeps slipping, too. I shall be getting a new car. At least, I think so. A Plymouth or a Jaguar or something. Let Austin have his swink to him reserved."

"I've got an Abelard. Second-hand."

"You'd better sell it. Quickly. There aren't many of those on the East Coast. There aren't any in Dahaga."

"What do you mean, sell it?"

"It's just down here," said Hardman. They passed attap shacks and many hens and naked cheerful children who cried, *"Tabek!"* in greeting. A goat bleated her flock off the road. "Hiya, kids," said Hardman. Soon they came to a lone bungalow with a back-cloth of swamp and coconut palms. The palms carried no fruit.

"Very bad soil," said Hardman. "Nothing grows here. A lot of malaria, too. It's those damned swamps. And then sand-fly fever. And snakes. And iguanas. Big ones."

"You make it sound most attractive," said Fenella. "And what does one do in the evenings?"

"Oh, there's a club. In town. But nobody ever speaks to

anybody there. It seems to be one of the rules. And you can go to the pictures. Indonesian epics and Indian visions of Baghdad, a very ill-lit Baghdad. It's best to stay at home and drink. Drink a lot. If you can afford it. Oh, you can bathe. But it's a bit treacherous. Look, this is where Talbot lives. Do you mind if I leave you here? He'll look after you. Actually, I don't particularly want to see his wife. Nor him, for that matter. Do look me up. At the Grand. And then we can talk. Soon, I think, I shall be able to buy you a beer. Perhaps two. At least, I hope so." He smiled at them wanly, reversed into a patch of coarse high grass, then bumped off back to the main road, his exhaust belching irritably.

"What a very extraordinary man," said Fenella. They stood on the bottom step of the bungalow, their luggage all about them.

"Oh, he's all right," said Crabbe. "You'll like him, once you get to know him. I wonder why he came out here."

"I wonder why anybody ever comes out here. I wonder why the hell we did."

"Never mind, darling." Crabbe took her arm, smiling ingratiatingly. The sun had started up again the gongs in his head, and the Lion-dance returned, twisting and jumping and bowing. But he felt hope, because he felt hungry. "Let's go and see if anybody's at home. Perhaps they'll give us something to eat."

So he knocked on the wooden wall beside the open door and braced himself to enter the life of the State of Dahaga.

2

"You see," he said, in sudden irritation, "they're still here. Spite of their bloody promises. Every day it's the same. You and me working our guts out in the sun, and them there in their motor-cars, going off to drink their whisky under a big fan." The brown, lined, lean workman leant on his heavy road-tool, whatever it was, and gawped indignantly at the passing car. His companion spat on to the scorched road and said, "They've let us down. They said when they got in there wouldn't be a white man left in the country. They said they'd all be buried alive." He spoke a thick strangulated Malay dialect, the tongue of Dahaga.

"Burnt alive."

"And now they've been in power since last August, and the white men are still here."

"Like what I said at first. They're still here."

"You can't trust the political men. Ties round their necks and kissing the babies. Promise you this and promise you that. And the white men are still here."

"Still here. Like what I said."

"I reckon we've done enough work for one day. We're only working for them." The car had long passed, but he spat in its direction, and the spit was swallowed by the large afternoon heat.

"I reckon we ought to lay off now."

A fat Tamil overseer came over to them, speaking toothy Malay, the Malay of the Tamils of another State, Greek to these workmen. Behind him the heavy steam-roller gleamed in gold of a Victorian coat-of-arms and seethed in boiling impotence. The two workmen listened stolidly, understanding one word in ten, understanding clearly the drift of the whole speech. When he had gone one said to the other:

"In the other States it's the Tamils does the dirty work."

"So they ought, black sods. Adam's shit, my father used to call them."

"Drunk on toddy every night."

"I reckon we ought to do a bit more and then lay off."

"All right. Till that monkey's finished throwing those nuts down from that tree over there. And then lay off."

They watched for a moment a *berok,* or coconut monkey, hurling down nuts to its master. The master gave it sharp orders, telling it only to pick the young soft-fleshed nuts. With an ill grace it obeyed. Languidly the two workmen pounded the road with their heavy tools, whatever they were called, the loose ends of their head-cloths agitated by the faint breeze.

The white man in the car sped on towards the town. Rupert Hardman was very much a white man, and all too aware of it. His skin was deficient in pigment, but only in moments of extreme depression, when pale eyes stared back bitterly from the mirror, did he call himself an albino. He was not quite that, there was just a rather unusual deficiency in pigmentation. A day on the beach and his thin body grew angry and peeled in its rage. His face grew tatters of curling white-tipped scarf-skin. His body, in spite of himself, sheered away from the sun as a cat, stiff with distended claws, sheers away from bath-water.

Perhaps it was only right that, nature having done one thing, war should finish things off. Rupert Hardman fingered with his left hand the skin around his nose and mouth. It was an old habit, ten years old. He had crashed towards the end of the war and his face had been ravaged by fire. The white man had been burnt alive. He still remembered the smell of the Sunday roast, he the joint, the cockpit the oven. Walking down the English suburban street, after eleven o'clock mass, with doors open to the warm family dinner smell, had always brought it back, and he had regularly escaped to the pub, just open at twelve, to drink cold beer. They said the doctors had done a marvellous job. The nurses cooed, perhaps a bit too much. When he plunged into the mirror he had not been displeased. Could you call it Rupert Hardman? That didn't seem to matter. It was an acceptable face, especially under the peaked officer's cap which hid the pale hair. And then leave.

In the village pub, the silly girl had greeted him and said:

"Ow, what's happened to you? You look like you've torn your fice and sewn it up yourself. Ever so funny."

But Crabbe hadn't looked as if he'd noticed. Crabbe had never noticed very much, though, the world of sensory phenomena meaning less to Crabbe than the world of idea and speculation. So it had been at the University, when Hardman, in his first year, had gone to hear Crabbe talk to the Communist Group, Crabbe the well-known and brilliant, for whom everyone prophesied a First. Crabbe had had no interest in the coming revolution, no love for the proletariat, only an abstract passion for the dialectical process, which he applied skilfully to everything. But Crabbe, as Hardman remembered, had been interested in a girl: a dark girl, small, usually dressed in a jumper and a tweed skirt, animated, talented, a student of music. Surely Crabbe had intended to marry this girl? Surely, now he came to think of it, Crabbe did marry this girl, during the war? Yet this woman whom he had met today, introduced as Mrs. Crabbe, was tall and fair and vaguely patrician. Not, thought Hardman, really Crabbe's type at all. This chance meeting stirred up the whole past in Hardman's mind as he drove expertly on to the town. The palm trees and the brown bodies and the China Sea became, despite the years of familiarity, suddenly strange, genuinely exotic, and he saw himself from the outside, driving a car in a Malay State to a Malay town, having spent the night in another Malay town where he had conducted the defence in a Malayan court, his home Malaya, his income —such as it was—derived from Malayan clients, wondering how the hell all this had happened, what he was doing here anyway, and thinking, with a sudden start of sweat that had nothing to do with the heat, that he was really imprisoned here, couldn't raise a passage to England, and if he returned there what was he to do anyway?

Yet Crabbe had brought back a whiff of nostalgia. Old oak in cool musty chambers, periodicals that were press-wet, not five weeks late, the queue for the ballet, a live orchestra, draught beer, ice on the roads and not just in the ice-box. Europe. "Better fifty years of Europe than a cycle of Cathay." That was Tennyson. It would have done that bearded gin-guzzling shag-smoking laureate of the antimacassars a lot of good to come out here and . . .

Cycles along Jalan Laksamana, main street of Kenching, and there the Cathay Cinema advertising an Indonesian film called *Hati Ibu*—'A Mother's Heart'. A huge brown weeping face and, in the background of the poster, the rising generation in jeans and Hawaiian shirts, off for a spree, forgetting the old ways, unmoved by a mother's tears. In the next-door kiosk a sulky ripe Malay girl offered lottery tickets for sale. Sweat shone on the lean shoulders of a turbaned fisherman, his silver-gleaming catch hanging from a pole. There was loud leisurely chaffering in the market over rambutans, aubergines, red and green peppers, Chinese oranges, white cabbages, dried fish-strips and red-raw buffalo-meat. The smells rose into the high blue coastal air. Hardman turned left and made for the Grand Hotel, and the reek of the river greeted him.

He wondered what it would feel like to be a Muslim, even in name only, and what sort of a life he could have with her. He seemed to be letting Europe down. Was it for this that the Crusades had been fought and Aquinas had tamed the Aristotelian beast into a *Summa*? But money was more important than faith. At least, now it was. Faith could come later.

In the hotel Auntie's husky whisky-bloom bass boomed down the telephone. She stood, as though speaking down the telephone in a play, on a kind of dais before an audience of Asian tea-drinkers. She had a vast flattened bosom and red hanging jowls and, as she spoke, her fat shook.

"I have my way to pay too. I have my creditors to meet. If you cannot afford to drink then you should not drink. Besides, it is forbidden by your religion to drink. That makes it all the more worse that you should run up debts. I know, I know. At the end of last month you promise me too. And now it is the end of another month. I have it here." She intoned to the tea-drinkers: "Che Abdul Kadir bin Mohamed Salleh. Haji Ali College. One hundred and fifty-five dollars." The tea-drinkers listened, the slightest pain of sympathy in their eyes. One or two men took down the name on cigarette packets. Blackmailers? Agents of the Supreme Council of Islam?

"Tomorrow," said Auntie. "Tomorrow at the latest. There are men up the road with little axes. They are only too glad to earn two, three dollars. To them to strike a man with an axe, it is nothing. It is to them an honest living." Calmly she put down the receiver. Her turtle-lidded eyes caught Rupert Hardman escaping up the stairs.

"Mr. Hardman."

"Oh, hello, Auntie." Rupert Hardman turned at the stair-head, a great nervous boyish smile on his thin face.

Auntie's heart melted, as it always did. Her huge body seemed to sag at the joints, as with incipient fever. "I will come up," she said, "just for a moment."

She mounted the stairs, pausing at each step, pausing at each phrase. "All the time money trouble. That is the big disease of Malaya. Not TB. Not malaria. And you are as bad." The banister groaned. "As the rest."

"Everything's going to be all right, Auntie. Just wait, that's all."

"I wait. I go on waiting. I think I wait too long."

Rupert Hardman entered his little room and switched on the bedside fan. The blades whirred comfortingly and coolly and the upper structure of the fan moved sedately from side to side, shedding coolness with royal bounty, now here, now there, crassly impartial. Hardman lay on the bed and looked up at the new blue distemper of the ceiling.

"You do not take off your shoes," said Auntie, entering. "You put dirt on the bed. That makes a lot of laundry."

"You always tickle my feet."

"There were perhaps men who were glad to have their feet tickled by me." Auntie lowered her bulk on to the single chair.

"When was that, Auntie, and where was that? When you danced the czardas with Admiral Horthy? When Petrograd was a snowy furry fairyland?"

"And what is to become of me here, sixty already, and nothing saved up, and the bills coming in and nobody paying their bills?"

"Blistered in Brussels, patched and peeled in London? Or nothing so exotic. Say, after *schnapps* and *rijstafel* in some Djakarta joint. I want to sleep. I've had a tiring two days. And I've eaten nothing."

"How can you eat when you pay no bills? Credit does not last for ever."

"Auntie," said Hardman, "I shall pay my bill." He suddenly felt hopeless and excited. "In full. And then it is quite certain that I shall go somewhere where they are not always asking for money. Somewhere where they will give me money."

"There." She came over and sat at the foot of the bed. "You get worried. I do not forget what Redshaw and Tubb did for me in Singapore. They are a very good firm. It is such a pity you got out of them. You would now be sitting pretty."

"They were a lot of blasted rogues. Sharp practice. I don't want to talk about them."

"And so. Because they get me off they are a lot of blasted rogues. So." Auntie rang the bell on the wall by the bed.

"It's not that. I'm not concerned with morals. Not as a lawyer. If you wanted to run what you did run it's your own affair. I suppose it's as honest as anything else."

"What I did run?" Auntie let out a pint of indignant air. "It was legitimate business. I only say you were a fool to get out of a firm like that. To be a lawyer on your own, that needs money. You have to have an office. How can you afford an office when you cannot pay my bills even?"

"I shall pay my bills. I shall get an office. And very soon. God help me."

"These two days then, you have been getting money?"

"Yesterday," said Rupert Hardman, incisively, forensically, "I had a case down south in the State of Kelantan, in the chief town of Kota Bharu. There, Auntie, I met nice people and stayed in a nice hotel kept by a very nice Russian lady, a lady who said I need not hurry about paying my bill, because she knew of my great ability and said that my credit was good. The case I had was a case of rape. It was a small Chinese shopkeeper who had taken advantage of one of his Malay assistants. I tell you this to prove to you that I have briefs. That means fees. But I cannot force my clients to pay any quicker than they wish to pay. One must be leisurely in these matters. One must give the impression that one can wait for ever for the fees."

"Yes, yes," said Auntie, soothingly. There was a knock at the door. "Come in," she called. "I mean, *masok.*"

Rupert Hardman laughed, his good humour somewhat restored. The Chinese Number One boy came in. "Whisky," said Auntie.

"And a raw beef sandwich," added Hardman. "*Masok,*" he laughed. At the door the boy hesitated. "No, no, no," said Hardman, "I didn't mean you." The boy went out. "I meant this case of rape. The prosecution went on about had he done this and had he done that, and had there been any attempt to, shall we say, force his attentions on her, and had he perhaps been importunate in demanding

25

her favours, and had there finally, let me see, this is most embarrassing, had he, shall we say, succeeded, if one may use the term, in effecting, let us say, any degree of penetration. The interpreter listened very patiently and then he just asked the girl, '*Sudah masok?*' and she replied, quick as a flash, '*Sudah.*' "

"*Masok!*" shrieked Auntie, all trembling jelly. The boy was standing patiently with the drinks. "*Sudah masok,*" he said patiently.

"Yes, yes, yes." Auntie coughed gargantuanly. "Now you can go out."

"Raw beef sandwiches," said Rupert Hardman, "with a raw onion."

Auntie turned to Hardman, came closer, put a huge mottled paw on his thin ankle. "It is not that I mind about the money. Your money, to me it means nothing. I am always grateful to Redshaw and Tubb."

"But I'm no longer with Redshaw and Tubb."

"Yes," said Auntie vaguely. "I see that. But there are so many ways in which you can help me. You are a young man of education. You are friendly with many Europeans."

"That's not going to count much from now on. Expatriates are going to have their throats cut."

"Ach." Auntie frowned hugely. "That is all nonsense. The Europeans will never go."

"They said that in Indonesia. Look at it now." Rupert Hardman poured water from the thermos jug into his whisky. "Where the hell are my sandwiches?" He petulantly drank the sharp cool potion.

"For example, you know women. Nice women. Women who are well-dressed and of education."

"Yes, Auntie?" Hardman looked up at her, smiling sweetly, gently.

"And gentlemen, of course. We want nice people to come here. There are nice business men who come from Bangkok, they want to meet nice people. Nice English people."

"Yes, Auntie."

"This could be a nice place. People drinking cocktails and laughing and talking very gay. Refined dinner-parties. And dancing to the radiogram."

"And nice refined seduction afterwards?"

Auntie boiled with large sudden anger. "Ach. You have only dirty thoughts in your mind. About me you have always had such thoughts."

"No, Auntie," said Hardman, sweetly, seriously. "I really and truly haven't."

Auntie smiled roguishly, hideously, and tweaked Hardman's ankle. "You are a bad boy," she said.

The boy came in with the sandwiches. Hardman devoured them wholemeal, munching with the swollen cheeks of a child. Auntie said, "You eat only sandwiches. Tonight you must eat a hot meal, with a spoon. There is chicken curry. With *gula Melaka* to follow."

"I shall eat out."

"You will not get much to eat with what you have in your pockets."

"There are many places where they're only too pleased for me to run up bills."

The Number Two boy came in to say that the Crown Prince was on the telephone. Something about a *mah jong* game. Auntie said, "Ach," and made her fat stately way to the door. "At least," she said, turning, "you are not in debt to me for *mah jong*. That is more than the Crown Prince can say."

When she had gone Hardman took off his clothes and

27

slept restlessly for an hour or two. He could hear clearly through his dreams the quarrelling of the Chinese couple in the next room, the crying of a child opposite, the oscillations and intermittent bursts of Hindi song from the radio down the corridor. His dreams were vague and historical. He was the Saracen spy in the entourage of Richard Cœur de Lion. He was a Spanish propagandist of the subtle doctrines of Averroes. As he was waking in the rose of the brief evening he was the muezzin announcing that there was no God but Allah. But the muezzin was outside, calling the sunset prayer from the loudspeaker opposite the Bank. He remembered he had an appointment, so he arose, showered his meagre body, and changed his trousers and shirt. He also put on a tie, remembering that he was an Englishman in the tropics. He was not in the Colonial Service, but he was still a white man. A very white man.

Early dusk was on the town. Hardman crossed the road, dodging trishaws and homeward cycles. He sought a drinking *kedai*, climbing steps to reach the high covered pavement that was snug above the flood-level. The monsoon was far off, months and months of sun stretched before him, heat in which the fine logic of the law-books would blur. But he would soon, he hoped, be settled in, with a name-plate outside and the law-books gathering mould on their shelves, litigation creaking on under the heavy indifferent rains or the big brassy law-abiding sun.

The *kedai* was gloomy, empty save for the man that Hardman had arranged to meet. The creased moon-faced Chinese grinned above his glass of beer at the marble table. The table bore a saucer of small bananas and a smoky glass case of pastries. The big beer-bottle was half-full and the Chinese called for another glass.

"Have you decided about the rent?" asked Hardman.

"Thirty-five dollars a week."

"That's a bit heavy. After all, the position isn't all that good."

"Lawyers make much money."

"This one doesn't."

"And also two thousand key-money."

"That's a bit thick."

"I should ask three thousand."

"It's not strictly legal, you know, to ask anything. You should be satisfied with a month's rent in advance."

"That is what is usually done. It is the custom. Custom is a kind of law."

"But two thousand dollars!"

"I have many inquiries about the shop. There were two men around today. One said he was very interested and would talk about it with his wife and see me tomorrow."

Rupert Hardman sipped his beer. It tasted very bitter. He owed three months' rent for Club chambers in Kuala Lumpur. He owed for his car. He owed various hotel bills. He had spent too much money on a girl called Enid.

"You wish not to take the premises?"

"No. Yes. Wait." Hardman looked at the small quizzical eyes, Chinese eyes, eyes of an alien code of ethics, eyes he could look at but never look into. Better fifty years of Europe. "I'll come and see you tomorrow. Early. I think I'll be taking the premises. It's a question of getting the money together."

"Cash."

"Hung," said a voice like a gong. "Hardman, you bastard." A small brown man with huge teeth and a wide-gated moustache was upon him, embracing him with loving arms and a rough cheek. It was Haji Zainal Abidin.

29

"Hardman, the bastard," he announced, "who threw the Koran on the floor and put his heel on it. The man with no respect for another man's religion."

"That's not true," said Hardman. "You threw it on the floor yourself. You said the Koran was too sacred to be translated. You said an English Koran was blasphemy. You stamped on it."

"No respect for another man's religion," said Haji Zainal Abidin. "He has seen the light. I have shown him the light. But still he has a prepuce." He laughed raucously, showing a red throat and uncountable teeth. "That is a good word," he said. "I said that today to my boss. 'Mr. Cheesy,' I said, 'the time is coming when there will be no prepuces left in our country. The prepuces,' I said, 'will be sent home with their owners.' 'And what is a prepuce?' he said." Haji Zainal Abidin laughed loud and harsh. "To think that I speak the white man's tongue better than the white man."

"On a point of anatomical fact," said Hardman, "I have no prepuce. It was removed when I was a child."

Haji Zainal Abidin sulked for an instant. Then he recovered and, in great good humour, introduced a dim Indian who had entered with him. The Indian was smiling and very drunk.

"This is my colleague," said Haji Zainal Abidin. "It is his day off today and he tries to spend it in his usual manner. He becomes drunk and he goes and buys things. Fortunately today is Chinese New Year and many shops are closed. But he has already bought two refrigerators, a radiogram and a Sunbeam Talbot. He has signed cheques for all these things and he has not two cents to rub together. But the men in the shops mostly know him now. Today it was mostly the assistants he saw, because the towkays were away drinking. But I have been round and got back the cheques. One day he will find it very difficult. Two years ago they deliver a bulldozer to him and he says he knows nothing about it. That will happen again, only perhaps that time it will be a cinema."

Haji Zainal Abidin did not proclaim, either in dress or demeanour, the pentecostal grace that traditionally descends on one who has made the pilgrimage to Mecca. He wore no turban, a natty cravat with a horse-head pin was tucked inside his open nylon shirt, his flannel trousers were well-creased and his shoes highly polished. He exhaled a heartening smell of hops, hardly concealed by the breath of garlic. He was in his late forties and depressingly vigorous. He called for beer. Mr. Hung said he had to be going.

"Tomorrow," said Hardman.

"You owe him money," shouted Haji Zainal Abidin. "Everybody owes Hung money."

"I want to open up an office," said Hardman. "That's all."

Haji Zainal Abidin became serious, confidential. "Money," he said. "You need money. I know." He leaned over, pushing a great nose, great eyes and the cleft in his moustache into the face of Hardman. "I have told you, there is only one way."

"I know. I've thought about it. I've been thinking about little else."

"What is holding you back?"

"You know what's holding me back. Or rather, what's been holding me back."

"There you go again," raged Haji Zainal Abidin. "Because she is a Malay. Race prejudice. Race hatred. I tell you again, you English bastard, there will be no peace

31

on the earth until race hatred ceases. Because you are a white man you despise us. You despise me because I am a Malay. You call me a Malay bastard. Well, I am not a Malay. I am an Afghan." He sat back in triumph. The dim Indian began to sing quietly to himself.

"It's not that. You know it's not that, you silly Afghan bastard."

Haji Zainal Abidin roared with great laughter. Then he said, "She is a young woman. She is only forty-two. And as for her other two husbands, you need not believe the stories. They were both estate-managers. It is highly probable that the Communists killed them. If you are a good husband to her, there is nothing she will not do for you. Nothing." He winked hugely, seriously. "She has money."

"It surprises me that nobody has snapped her up already," said Hardman. "You, for instance. You've only got one wife at the moment."

Haji Zainal Abidin leaned forward, froth on his lips, his face a devil's mask of cunning, his teeth set as though he carried a knife between them. "I have had four wives," he said. "I have fourteen, fifteen children. I am not sure of the number. Of these wives only my first wife is left. She is the only woman for me. Late, I realised that she was always that. She has had staying-power. She is the only woman in the world for whom I have any appetite. Any *appetite*." He bit off the word itself with something like appetite. Hardman felt his own saliva stir. "There are no women like the Arab women," said Haji Zainal Abidin dreamily, lyrically. "No women for beauty or fidelity. She was twelve when I first met her in her father's house, with her dark eyes flashing like fire above the veil. That was in Mecca itself. She is not only a child of Mecca but a lady of the line of the Prophet. A lady, yes. More of a lady

32

than these Malay women, who are no true Muslims. They walk about in their powder and high heels, drinking beer publicly. They have no shame."

"There's no way out, is there?" said Hardman. "If I marry her I'll have to enter Islam."

"And why should you not?" stormed Haji Zainal Abidin. "It is the true religion, you Christian bastard. It is the only one. The rest are mere imitations."

"Oh, you just don't understand." Hardman felt hopeless again. Soon he said, "You'll have to help me find a name. A Muslim name."

"It is a pleasure," said Haji Zainal Abidin. "It is my duty, too, for you are my friend. You shall become also my son in God. You shall be Abdullah bin Haji Zainal Abidin. No, no. There are better names than Abdullah. I must think of a really good one." He thought.

"Tonight, then," said Hardman, "I shall propose."

"There are many good names. I was just going through the names of my sons. I cannot remember them all. Latif? Redzwan? Redzwan is a good name. It means grace."

"I can't be called Grace. That's a girl's name."

"You shall be called what I say," Haji Zainal Abidin nudged the Indian, his sleeping partner. "Wake up! This is a solemn moment."

"I shall go round to her house after dinner," said Hardman with gloom.

"We shall all go," cried Haji Zainal Abidin. "We shall have a party. We shall go round and collect the others. We shall buy beer. We shall call for Kadir first. He has a motor-cycle and sidecar. Kadir is a good name. Abdul Kadir. You shall be called Abdul Kadir. Abdul Kadir bin Haji Zainal Abidin. That shall be your name."

"LL.B. Barrister-at-law. A bit of a mouthful."

33

"Let us go," said Hardman's father in God. He stood up and seized his Indian friend by the scruff. The Indian woke smiling. "This is a great occasion. An infidel has been called home to the true way. Allah be praised." He drained his beer standing, sighed with satisfaction, banged down the tall glass. He led the way out, singing in a thin muezzin's wail.

Rupert Hardman followed him into the dim-lit dark, Abdul Kadir bin Haji Zainal Abidin, heir to two cultures. Allah be praised.

3

"There must be somebody at home," said Fenella. "There's a car."

"A Land Rover."

"Try again."

Crabbe rapped once more, but the faint wooden noise seemed swallowed by vast Malayan distances, and they became oppressed by a great loneliness. The lizards darted into familiar sand-holes; the sun howled down; a distant goat wavered a plaintive call. Things went indifferently on, and nobody wanted the Crabbes. Perhaps they, like their side-walking namesakes, should dig holes and then bed down in sight of the vast empty sea, rejected of the warm-blooded inland world. But Victor Crabbe decided on action. He walked into the house and looked shyly round a large sitting-room, all buff-painted wood, pictures, mats, gin-tables, books, Trengganu fans, Kelantan silver, empty chairs. Uncertainly he called: "Is anyone at home?"

The silence chewed this over. Then, sluggishly, the emptiness stirred itself into movement. A door opened, one of the three doors that presumably led to bedrooms. A man, appeared, wearing the uniform of the Home Guard, three stars on his shoulders. He was dark-haired, moustached, big, his face a cliché of handsomeness— straight nose, cleft chin, deep brown humorous eyes, small ears, a healthy tan: a face no intelligent woman would look at twice. Crabbe could see that the uniform had only recently been reassumed: there was a certain carelessness about buttons, the shorts were somewhat baggy, the hair had been hurriedly welshcombed. He listened with sympathy to the soft Scottish voice.

"Would you be looking for Talbot? He's not normally back till about three. Mrs. Talbot will be coming out in a wee while. She and I have been rehearsing a scene from a play that we're going to do. We were shouting a wee bit, so we couldn't have heard you knock. Just arrived, I suppose? I'm Bannon-Fraser."

Hand-shakes. Bannon-Fraser smiled with interest at Fenella. "We don't see many fair-haired ladies out here," he said, "not nowadays. You've probably heard all about that."

"No," said Fenella, "I haven't."

"Oh," said Bannon-Fraser, "it's the Abang. You've heard about the Abang?"

"I've read about him," said Crabbe. "At least, I've read about the office, the Abang-paradigm, you might say. What has the Abang got to do with fair-haired women?"

"What's he got to do?" Bannon-Fraser laughed, showing, inevitably, strong white teeth. "What's he got to do with fair-haired women? He loves 'em, laddie, can't have too many of them." The schoolboy salacity disappeared from his look. Seriously he said to Fenella, "I'm sorry. I shouldn't have said that. You're in Education, aren't you? Well, you'll be all right, I suppose. It's only at the Drainage and Irrigation level that he starts any funny business. Or Agricultural Department. Of the earth earthy. I should think Education's a bit outside his scope. I've got to go now. Mrs. T. will be up, out, any minute now. Do come round to the mess sometime. Or see you at the club. We'll have a drink," he added, as though this thought were a sudden inspiration. Then he left with the hurry of a man who has fulfilled a duty that, with the long passage of time, has become more and more perfunctory, a function that has developed economy of action, a routine as gratifying as the fiftieth cigarette of the day. Crabbe and Fenella decided to sit down, hearing the Land Rover roar away up the road.

There was a picture on the wall that caught Crabbe's attention, an obviously amateur picture. Female breasts, greatly elongated, grew up, tufted like brushes at the points, into a forest. The dendromorphs were painted in nursery colours, like children's beakers. Crabbe's appetite receded. Fascinated, he looked at others: a snake entering a woman's mouth; a stylised satyr leaping out of a cuplike navel; a parade of pink haunches. Each picture carried the bold vermilion initials: A.T. Soon they were both wandering about the room, colliding at intervals and saying, "Sorry."

"Trying to shock," said Fenella, as the two of them craned at a sort of erotic Laocoon, poster-paint flesh and ill-proportioned limbs. "He wants everybody to think he's interestingly depraved. It's all very childish."

"You don't have to look at them," said a voice. They turned guiltily. "I do these for my own amusement." The speaker lounged at the bedroom door, her mouth wagging a cigarette. She was slim and seemed to be wearing a sort of ballet practice dress. Her face was that of a boy gang-leader, smooth with the innocence of one who, by the same quirk as blinds a man to the mystery of whistling or riding a bicycle, has never mastered the art of affection or compassion or properly learned the moral dichotomy. Her

37

eyes were small and her lips thin, her black hair parted demurely in Madonna-style. Her voice was faint, as if her vocal cords had been eroded by some acid. Crabbe suddenly heard the voice of a Malay girl who, a year ago, had enticed him from a lonely roadside: *"Tuan mahu main-main?"* But *Tuan* had not wanted to play: in the strained whisper spoke the aristocratic disease of love.

"I'm Anne Talbot," she said. "I suppose you must be expected or something. My husband never tells me anything. Please sit down, both of you." Fenella flushed: she had not stood up, she had merely been standing. She remembered vaguely a film about a Restoration trollop promoted to duchess: "No ceremony here, ladies." She did not sit down until she had finished counting fifty. The counting also kept her mouth shut.

Crabbe announced his name and, for some reason, suddenly felt ashamed of it. It carried the wrong connotations—crustaceans, pubic parasites, instead of innocent wild apples.

"Crabbe," said Mrs. Talbot. "Crabbe. That's a nice name. It reminds me of wild apples." (I was wrong, he thought, in thinking them innocent.) "I used to be very fond of crab-apple jelly, back in England, of course, when I was a young girl. I never get it now. Never. There are a lot of things I don't get." She leaned back in her armchair and blew smoke feebly. "One becomes so very tired of it all."

Fenella was now seated. She looked at Crabbe and Crabbe looked at the floor and both felt a slight chill of premonition adding its draught to that of the ceiling-fan. Crabbe felt also shame. All this had been set out years ago in the stories of a man still well remembered in the East. Willie Maugham, damn fine bridge-player, real asset to the club,

38

remembered me, put me in a book. Things here were all too simple. That Elizabethan play of adultery and jealousy, Fenella remembered, that play with the unironic title of *A Woman Killed with Kindness,* had reflected a civilisation a thousand times more complex. Fenella and Crabbe looked at each other briefly, and the business of the anonymous letter was already torn up.

"A drink," said Mrs. Talbot. "Our servants have taken the day off. I can't understand how two Malays could possibly have Chinese cousins, but that was their story, so off they've gone to celebrate the New Year. Perhaps you, Mr. Crabbe, would like to give us some gin and vermouth. It's all in that cupboard. And there's ice in the refrigerator."

"I don't particularly want a drink," said Fenella.

"Nor I," said Crabbe, "particularly."

"Well," said Mrs. Talbot, "I do." She gave Crabbe a five-second glance of her small eyes and a grimace of her thin red lips, then she shrugged her very thin shoulders, got up, and lounged to the drink-cupboard. Crabbe made a frog's mouth and slightly raised his hands at Fenella. Then a car-noise approached and was ground out in front of the bungalow. They both breathed relief. Heavy feet mounted and Crabbe rose.

"Don't tell me, don't tell me," said Talbot. "It's Bishop. We're back together again. God, it's been a long time. Mrs. Bishop, how are you? Young and beautiful as ever, despite the heavy weight of the years. And the other boys, how are they, Bishop?"

It was the moon-face of a yokel, a lock of straw-straight hair kissing one lens of the cheerful spectacles. The fleshy face and paunchy stumpy body, clad in a blue shirt and what looked like running shorts, spoke of a hopeless euphoria. Talbot seemed in his middle forties. He was evidently reaping the dank straw harvest of marrying a much younger wife. He was too cheerful. Soon, it was evident, he would talk with enthusiasm of his hobby, probably something laborious and harmless. The face was not that of a man of talent or temperament: it was too knobby and unlined, and the metal-gleaming teeth were too readily shown in an empty desperate smile.

"Crabbe," said Crabbe. "You may have had a letter about me."

"Crabbe," said Talbot. "I thought you were Bishop. You're very like Bishop. And of course there must be a connection somewhere. Let me see. Yes. Bishop was an eighteenth-century drink. Dr. Johnson was very fond of it. And you use crab-apples for making lamb's wool. That, you'll remember, was an Elizabethan drink. 'When roasted crabs hiss in the bowl.'" He made 'bowl' rhyme with 'owl'. "Or perhaps there was a Bishop Crabbe. There must be somewhere in Anthony Trollope. Are you any relation to the poet?"

"Distant. But my grandmother was a Grimes."

"Well, well." Talbot seemed pleased. "I suppose you've come to take over the College. I must say they've been pretty quick. Foss only went two days ago."

"They kept us hanging about for a month. Back in Kuala Hantu."

"Oh, God, that horrible place. Well, well. This calls for a drink. Anne, give us all a drink."

"They said they didn't want a drink. They were absolutely certain that they didn't want a drink." Mrs. Talbot came back with a full glass for herself.

"You see," said Crabbe, "it's the old business of an empty stomach."

"My dear fellow," said Talbot. He spoke as if Crabbe had committed a sin which was canonically mortal but because he, Talbot, was a Jesuit of the world, could be softened and attenuated till it disappeared like ectoplasm through the confessional grille. "My dear fellow." And then Crabbe knew what Talbot consoled himself with. The successful grew fat on plovers and cream; the unsuccessful on bread and jam and swigs from the custard-jug. "My dear fellow, you ought to eat. That's the trouble with my wife. Thin as a rake, because she won't bother to order anything. Says she's not hungry. I'm always hungry. This climate has different effects on different people. I always have my lunch out. There's a little Chinese place where they give you a really tasty and filling soup, packed with chicken and abalone and vegetables, with plenty of toast and butter, and then I always have a couple of baked crabs."

"Yes," said Crabbe.

"With rice and chilli sauce. And then a pancake or so, rather soggy, but I don't dislike them that way, with jam and a kind of whipped cream they serve in a tea-cup. Anne, what is there to eat?"

"There's nothing laid on, and the servants have gone. There, I'll give you that as a free gift. You can start writing an intelligible poem for a change."

Talbot laughed indulgently, as if to say, "Isn't she a one?" He turned adoringly to her and said, "There must be something in the larder. Dig something out."

"Crabs are good at digging," said Mrs. Talbot. "Perhaps Mr. Crabbe would like to help me."

"Yes, yes, do that, Crabbe. And then I can talk to Mrs. Bishop."

Crabbe and Mrs. Talbot entered the sun-hot store-room.

There were many tins and jars. "You can have cocktail sausages and gherkins," she said, "and tinned cheese and anchovies and pork-liver pâté. Or beetroot and Gentleman's Relish. We could have a little picnic. We could eat off the leaf, as the Malays say." She was not near him, but the hot room diffused her scent. If he were to kiss her now she would taste it as casually and dispassionately as a fingerful of Gentleman's Relish or a cold lean sausage. He remembered his hunger and said, "This, I think. And perhaps this."

"What a greedy boy you are. Just like Herbert. Come on then, let's empty things on to plates." She led him into the kitchen.

Sawing at bread she cut her finger. That was to be expected also. "Oh, look, blood! Dripping over everything. Oh dear, dear, I can't stand the sight of it." She danced prettily up and down, enticing him to say: "Poor little finger. Let me kiss the blood off."

"Run some water over it," said Crabbe.

"Oh, well, if it drips into the beetroot it won't show, will it? And nobody will know, will they? Except you and me." Crabbe felt curiously uneasy, as if the harmless canned provisions were the raw materials of necromancy. He remembered Dahaga's sinister reputation for magic, but then shook the silly fancy away. After all, it was her blood, not his.

When they got back to the lounge, carrying two trayloads of plates, they found Talbot in the middle of one of his own poems. He was intoning harshly and without nuances from a heavily corrected manuscript:

". . . Cracks open the leaden corncrake sky with crass,
    angelic

Wails as round as cornfruit, sharp as crowfoot, claw-
foot,
Rash, brash, loutish gouts of lime or vinegar strokes
Till the crinkled fish start from their lace of
bone. . . ."

Fenella sat with her head lowered, embarrassed. So
adolescent. And yet the theme was not the lustful itch of
adolescence. The subject was food, sheer food. It was a
picture of Talbot at breakfast or a chipped-potato supper.
Or probably all meals coalesced with him in an orgy of
thick bread-and-marge and an array of sauce-bottles. The
poem rang with the bells that called Pavlov's dogs to
salivation. Fenella was sensitive to the harmonics of words.
She was a poet herself.

Talbot looked up brightly at the loaded trays. "A bit
peckish," he said. "I had lunch early." Then he speared
a sausage and spooned out mixed pickles.

"Now," said Crabbe, "tell me all about it."

"Yes." Talbot caught a trio of sardines and bathed them
in pickle-sauce. "Yes. You mean about Haji Ali College?"

"Yes."

"Well, it was named after Haji Ali."

"One of the great men of the State?"

"Yes. I see you know all about it."

"No."

Talbot squirled a couple of anchovies in. "A hero chiefly
because he once cheated a Chinese shopkeeper. By God,
that takes some doing. But also he was a poor boy who
made good. He graduated from sneak-thief, axe-man and
occasional pirate to *haji*." The word *haji* seemed to induce
appetite in Talbot. He took in a dessertspoonful of
mustard pickle and continued through saffron lips: "He

43

reformed and determined that his last theft should enable him to make the pilgrimage. By God, he did it. He went to Mecca and came back with a turban. Then he became town magician and I gather he was pretty good. He cured the Sultan of . . ."

"Darling, not while our guests are eating."

"Anyway, when he died there was universal mourning. Drums going all night, black kids sacrificed to obscure Hindu gods. Then they started building this school. At first the idea was to call it after the Abang, but Haji Ali's ghost appeared to the workmen and things began to go wrong. You know the sort of thing—scaffolding rotting at the roots and the bricks condemned as pure jelly." Bewildered, Talbot looked around and finally lit on a jar of Brand's Chicken Essence. He poured some into tomato juice, added salt, and drank with a sigh. "Got to watch vitamins. Bulk isn't enough. That's where the Malays make a mistake. Rice, rice and more rice."

"But look at their waist-lines, dear."

"Anyway, to continue. The whole damn structure fell down, a month off opening day. A workman said that Haji Ali had appeared to him in a dream and sworn at him in Arabic. The workman said that he had had a vision—the school appeared as a vast fish curry at a huge feast of workmen. Then Haji Alil arrived, amid cheers, and he poured a sort of thin chutney over the whole thing. But the whole thing went up in smoke, leaving a big ruin of white rice. And the voice of the Lord was heard in a kind of stereophonic sound, saying: 'Woe to the children of the scripture, for their aspirations shall become as garlic on the wind.' And so they thought it better to re-name the College, and everything went right, and there's been no trouble since."

44

"Tell me about it," said Crabbe.

"Well." Talbot cut a slice of tinned cheese. "You've got about a thousand pupils and a staff of Malays, Indians, Chinese and Eurasians. They're all going to hate your guts, especially the Senior Master. He's a Tamil called Jaganathan, and he was definitely promised the headship when Foss went home. Of course, it was only an electioneering promise, and that sort of promise doesn't mean a thing, but these poor devils had never had an election before, and they genuinely believed all that stuff about cutting the white man's throat. Poor old Jaganathan drummed up a lot of votes for the man who made the promise about the headship, so you can understand how he's going to feel about you."

"It's hardly my fault, is it? People shouldn't make promises they can't keep. Besides, this Jaganathan doesn't sound too bright."

"He's not, but that doesn't matter. He's been in the college for fifteen years, he's got a lot of contacts, and he's well in with the local magic boys. You've heard about those?"

"A little. Do you mean he's going to stick pins in my image?"

"He might." Comfortably Talbot looked round the fast-emptying plates and finally settled on a huge red round of beetroot. He put this whole into his mouth. As he talked it lolled for a second or two like an extra tongue. Mrs. Talbot smiled grimly at Crabbe, and Crabbe began to feel warmer towards her. "Anyway, he's not a graduate. Of course, nobody sees that that's important. They all think that our skin is our only piece of parchment. We carry our whiteness like a diploma. I say, that's not bad. I can use that."

"And the house?" asked Fenella.

"It's a good house. The situation may seem rather peculiar, because it looks as though it's set in the middle of a *kampong*. But that was because of Foss. He used to encourage the Malays to come and sit on his veranda and he'd tell them stories about the great world beyond the seas. Foss was a bit touched. A bachelor, you know. Never drank, never went to the Club. He had a vision of himself as a kind of saviour of the down-trodden brown man. He gave money away right and left, and it wasn't long before the local Malays began to carry their houses and dump them down near his, so that he became the centre of a whole new *kampong*. You've seen them do that, have you? The whole damn village carrying a house on their shoulders, yelling like mad. They do it a lot round here. Portable *kampongs*."

"Perhaps now that we've come they'll carry them away again," said Crabbe.

"Well, that's up to you, old boy. You'll see them coming round tonight, ready for a bed-time story. I shouldn't give them the brush-off if I were you. They're a touchy lot and they carry axes."

"Look," said Fenella, "when's the next plane back?"

"But old Foss wasn't so Malay-struck that he didn't provide himself with one of the best Chinese cooks in the State. I've had some marvellous meals there. I tried to entice him away, but he wouldn't come. Says he's too old to start chopping and changing now. So he goes with the house."

"Do you mean to say that we have a first-class cook laid on?" said Crabbe.

"You're lucky, old man. Ah Wing is the goods. He's a bit cracked, of course, laughing away to himself all the time, and he's a bit deaf, so that it's no good giving him any orders. Just let him carry on in his own way, and you'll be more than satisfied."

"Well," said Crabbe. He sat back, dazed. "I can hardly wait."

"I'm going home," said Fenella. "I'm definitely going home. As soon as you can book me a passage."

"Don't talk like that," said Talbot, happy and replete. "You're going to love it here. You just wait and see."

"Just wait and see," said Mrs. Talbot with some bitterness. "It's a white woman's paradise."

"Well, if you'll forgive me," said Talbot, "I've got to be on my way. You know the tradition. Chinese New Year they like you to drop in and have the odd bite with them and a glass of whisky. I've got several calls to make. Do come and see us again when you're settled in. I must read you some more of my verse, Mrs. Bishop."

"Crabbe," said Fenella.

"I beg your pardon?" Talbot looked vaguely insulted.

"Can you take us to the house?" said Crabbe. "Our car's still on its way. Besides, we just don't know our way around." He glanced at Mrs. Talbot. "Topographically, I mean."

"Delighted," said Talbot. He went ahead, his plenilunar buttocks tight in the very short shorts. "This your luggage?"

"Thank you so much," said Crabbe, smiling with his mouth at Mrs. Talbot who lay languid in her armchair, "for your hospitality."

"Delighted," she said. "Any time. I like being hospitable."

4

'Che Normah binte Abdul Aziz was supervising the clearing-up after the party. It was a party that had ended early; the last maudlin protestations of eternal amity, the trite philosophisings, the long visits to the back-yard *jamban* rebuked by the false-dawn call of the muezzin. The clearing-up was prolonged and squeamish: there was much mess revealed by the sunlight. Abdul Kadir had tried to make things go, as he always did. He had emptied most of the bottled beer, a quart of stout, a flask of Beehive Brandy, half a bottle of Wincarnis and the remains of the whisky into a kitchen pail. He had seasoned this foaming broth with red peppers and invited all to drink deep. This had been his sole contribution to the victualling of the party. Cheerful, quarrelsome, always in working shorts, his crew-cut bullet-head rendered scholarly by rimless glasses, he was never solvent. He regularly apologised for the fact, calling at friends' houses to express regret for his inability to return past hospitality, continuing the apologies over the hastily-laid extra dinner-place, the beer that had to be sent for, forgetting the apologies over the final nightcap, when he would ask such provocative questions as: "What is religion?" "Why do we allow the white man to stay?" "Why cannot Islam develop a more progressive outlook?" It was such questions as these that slammed the cork in his host's bottle.

His friends were, in a distracted way, ashamed of him, but the shame was of such long standing that it had transmuted itself into a kind of special affection. His penury was looked upon as a sort of holy idiocy, and he was granted such privileges as swigging a whole bottle of Benedictine at a sitting, being sick in the ash-trays, using vile English obscenities he had learned in the Navy. Much could be excused him anyway, for he was no true Malay. He was a mixture of Arab, Chinese and Dutch, with a mere formal sprinkling of Malay floating, like those red peppers, on the surface. His friends, complacently pitying this eccentric product of miscegenation, would forget the foreign bodies in their own blood. Haji Zainal Abidin would cease to be mainly Afghan; 'Che Abdullah no longer spoke the Siamese he had sucked from his mother; little Hussein forgot that his father was a Bugis. When they talked about Malay self-determination, they really meant that Islam should frighten the Chinese with visions of hell; but perhaps they did not even mean that. They themselves were too fond of the bottle to be good Muslims; they even kissed women and ate doubtful meat. They did not really know what they wanted. The middle-class of Kenching who carried Muslim names and were not too dark, not too light, were united by the most tenuous of bonds. One of these bonds was 'Che Guru Abdul Kadir, the hairy-legged goat who carried their sins on his back, who defined a vague smoky image of the true Malay (who did not exist), the true Islam (not really desirable) in terms of what these things were not. Certainly a beer or two and an occasional Friday absention from mosque did not seem so heinous when Abdul Kadir lay cursing in his vomit.

'Che Normah wrinkled her flat splay nose in disgust as

the servant swabbed the doorstep. She liked a party, but she did not like a party to get out of hand. When she had been mistress of two rubber estates the parties had been more decorous: much whisky had been taken, ribald songs sung, but the white man usually knew when he had gone too far, he could usually be controlled. ('Che Normah knew a great deal about controlling white men.) Give a little alcohol, however, to men like Mat bin Hussein, Din, Ariffin, Haji Zainal Abidin, and you could always expect the worst. Here was the pretty Chinese table whose top had been greased smearily by the flat feet of Ariffin doing his little dance. There was the Persian carpet on which Din had allowed clumsily-opened beer to froth freely. Bits of broken glass lay about, ready to ambush bare feet. Even 'Che Isa, the normally lady-like colleague of the accursed Abdul Kadir, had behaved sillily, making up to married men. Only Rupert had been reasonably restrained. ('Che Normah pronounced the name in the Malay manner, metathetically: Ruperet, the final dental initiated but not exploded. She had been practising the name a lot lately.) But Rupert was a white man and could be controlled. A very white man. And to think that that fool of a *haji* had proposed naming him after that drunken improvident lout Kadir. Normah had put her foot down. He was to be called Abdullah. That was to be his mosque-name and his burial-name. In the house he was still to be called Ruperet.

'Che Normah was a good Malay and a good Muslim. That is to say, her family was Achinese and came from Northern Sumatra and she herself liked to wear European dress occasionally, to drink stout and pink gin and to express ignorance about the content of the Koran. The Achinese are proverbially hot-blooded and quick on the draw, but the only knives 'Che Normah carried were in her eyes and her tongue. She gave the lie to the European superstition—chiefly a missionary superstition—that the women of the East are down-trodden. Her two husbands—the first Dutch and the second English—had wilted under her blasts of unpredictable passion and her robust sexual demands. The Communist bullets that had rendered her twice a widow had merely anticipated, in a single violent instant, what attrition would more subtly have achieved.

Haji Zainal Abidin had been too cautious in telling Hardman that both had 'probably' been killed by Communists. There was no doubt about those two identical ends: tappers had stood open-mouthed and impassively around while execution had been performed. But possibly Haji Zainal Abidin had had in mind a subtler and more forensic question: that of ultimate responsibility. Macbeth had used no knife on Banquo, but he had none the less killed him. The Communist terrorists, whose trade was death, had frequently been known to put, at the request of tappers, an unpopular foreman out of the way. They were at times glad enough to be hired assassins and were content with a payment of rice and a few tins of corned beef. It might or might not be significant that both Willem Pijper and John Hythe had been shot a few days before they were due for repatriation. A Muslim marriage does not need a civil contract to make it legal in a Muslim state, but in a Christian country marriage is not marriage unless there be benefit of registrar. It is just possible that both Pijper and Hythe were frivolous in their attitude to marrying 'Che Normah, that they merely wanted, in the American phrase, to 'get shacked-up', and the Muslim names they assumed were an amusing fancy dress. But 'Che Normah was no Cho Cho San. Allah had spoken in the Communist rifle-shots, and 'Che Normah had become doubly a wealthy widow: bonuses lay snug in the Anglo-Chinese Bank, the rubber companies had paid handsome compensation, there had been life insurance. Now, mistress of a house that was her own, she contemplated marriage once again, perhaps for the last time. She had worked out details of the marriage contract herself and, if she was to pay heavily for Rupert Hardman, she was determined on getting her money's worth. It was promotion, this new marriage: Hardman was a professional man, not a glorified foreman. There would be invitations to the Residency on the Queen's Birthday, dances at the Club, the prestige of going about on the arm of a man whose untannable skin could not be mistaken for that of a Eurasian. John Hythe had—only once—come back drunk from the club to announce with passion that someone had called him a *Serani*. The brown face and arms of an open-air worker, the marriage to a Malay—the catty club-women had been only too ready to look for a touch of the tar-brush. He had stormed and volubly regretted his marriage and she had knifed him back with her more deadly tongue, ending by throwing a chair at him and then, excited, taking him to bed. Willem Pijper had indulged in no such cries of wounded blood: he probably had been Eurasian.

It was a good solid house, fanless but airy. As the servant cleaned up, 'Che Normah looked round its rooms with approval, not regretting the high price she had paid for it. Its view was good. From the porch she could see the Law Courts and the Bank and the Great Mosque, a piquant anthology of architectural styles: Colonial Palladian; a timid approach to Corbusier; Hollywood Alhambran. And there would be no question of her husband coming home smelling of chlorophyll tablets and pleading a long day in court. She would be able to see him going in and coming out. The office was a different matter: that was to be on Jalan Laksamana, but Jalan Laksamana was full of her spies. 'Che Normah went to the back door and looked out on her cool garden: a rain-tree and a flame-of-the-forest, gaudy Malayan flowers that officials of the Agricultural Department had, as a labour of love, classified in cold Latin, but to which liberal peasants had given grosser names, names which 'Che Normah hardly knew, for all flowers with her were subsumed in the general term *bunga*. For her only the life of the flesh was important. At her feet was a clump of the leaves called touch-me-not, leaves which pretended death and curled up at the approach of foot or hand. For some reason, seeing them do this, 'Che Normah smiled secretly.

'Che Normah was a handsome woman. (Another smug European fallacy is that Eastern women lose their beauty quickly.) 'Che Normah was forty-two, but her hair was lustrous under its perm, her coffee skin smooth, eyes large, chin firm. She was lavish in build, with great thighs but a slim waist, bathycolpous as any Homeric heroine. Her walk evoked images from such Malay poets as had felt the influence of the Persians: melons in the melon-season, twin moons that never waned (but, she ensured, never waxed either.) She ate sparsely of rice but was fond of salads of cucumber, lady's fingers and red peppers, a little tender meat from Singapore Cold Storage, the choicer kinds of sea-food. She ate only when she was hungry. She could dance but played no games. She knew some Dutch and spoke a high-pitched stressless English. Her Malay was the Malay of the State of Lanchap, the State where, to use the idiom, her blood had first been poured, and she spoke it fierily, with crisp glottal checks, with much bubbling reduplication. (Optionally, Malay repeats words to express plurality and intensity. The connotations of both these terms were appropriate to 'Che Normah.)

Today her betrothed had a case in court. The court, she knew, rose for tiffin at twelve-thirty, and soon it would be time for her to watch him come out, thin and very white, elegant enough in unpaid-for palm-beach suiting. (So many bills of his had to be paid; well, she would pay them.) She was prepared, until the marriage contract had actually been signed, to forgo her proleptic right to control his movements and associations. There was plenty of time. But, almost sentimentally, she wanted to rehearse the part of the doorstep-waiting wife, the hand waving at the approaching lean figure, the white boyish face perhaps breaking into a smile of greeting. Realistic like all Achinese, she knew that the greeting smile would not last for long, or, if it did last, it would become twisted. But she tried to retain this rare mood of sentimentality, even tried to intensify it by applying it to the past as well as the future, and so went for her photograph album and sat down, barefooted, on the step.

Studio photographs: herself in rich Malay dress; in a frothy evening frock; a profile with bare brown shoulders. And the innumerable snapshots: herself and a Japanese girl-friend in pre-war Singapore; a group on the estate, her doomed Dutchman next to her; herself in bathing costume, leaning back provocatively in the sun; a Chinese dinner, with her second husband fumbling chopsticks to his mouth; Willem smiling vacantly, an arm about her. The sentimental mood did not last. Her eyes hardened.

Soon she brought to the door-step a plate of cold curried beef, fiery pepper-choked fibres, and forked it in delicately. Then, unaware of irony, she hummed "One Fine Day" while picking her teeth. "A man, a little man, is approaching across the *padang*." She did not know the words.

Before twelve-thirty the court recessed. She saw her betrothed come out, talking to a white-suited Tamil, making forensic gestures, his brief under his arm. Then she saw him prepare to move off and then someone come on to the scene up left, and accost him gently.

The storms began to stir in her eyes, for, despite everything, she was still a daughter of Islam, and the man that Rupert Hardman was talking to was just the man he should not be talking to. She banged her fist on the empty curry plate and it cracked in two.

5

Having telephoned his client, still waiting at the Club, to say that his case (breach of contract, brought by a servant) would not now come up till the afternoon, Rupert Hardman left the court-house, wiping irritably his face and the back of his neck, his brief under his arm, listening to the chatter of the Tamil interpreter whose name he had forgotten. Chinese cases are brisk, the litigants want to get back to business, but with Indians there is an unhealthy love of the law, and a petty case of the theft of ten dollars had evoked high drama—wailings, rendings of shirts already rent, flashing eyes and poetry, babies exhibited theatrically at moments of crisis. The case was likely to eat away a great deal of the afternoon—because of a certain dramaturgical rhythm its length could roughly be judged —and certainly the audience would not object. The law was a poor man's circus and the public benches were crammed with *aficionados* of the short answer and the long answer, the crescendo and the climax, the thumping of breast and elevation of eyes, the tears and the hard-luck story.

"Our worthy magistrate," said the Tamil interpreter, "is too enamoured with the niceties of English idiom. He told the Chinese defendant that he would let him off this time but that henceforth he must paddle his own canoe. Our friend Wong translated this for him too literally, saying that the defendant must expiate his crime by taking a sampan up and down the river. Whereupon the defendant said he would take anything but a sampan, anything—a fine of a thousand dollars, a week's gaol—but how could he now, at his age, forsake his business and become a sampan-man. You see thus the stupidity of the Malays. A Malay magistrate takes everything too far, including the English language, and our worthy 'Che Yunus is no exception to the rule."

Hardman nodded, remembering that 'Che Yunus had reviled a Tamil witness, a convert to Islam, because he gave his name as Abdullah bin Abdullah. Had he no imagination, did he think so little of the faith he had entered as to take the most obvious, the least inspiring name that came to hand? 'Che Yunus was ready to dismiss him from the witness-stand, as a man without a name, until counsel had gently intervened.

'Che Normah had decreed that Rupert Hardman's new name should be Abdullah bin Abdullah.

Hardman now became irritable and expressed impatience at the long waiting in the heat, the frivolous attitude of the East to the calm processes of Western Law. He waved his arm in a gesture of weariness. The Tamil nodded, saying: "It is the heat, Mr. Hardman. It is getting you down. How long since you have had leave?"

"Leave? How can I afford leave?"

"Soon, I hear, you will be able to afford it. But will you then be able to take it?"

Hardman did not answer. There were obviously no secrets in this town. Haji Zainal Abidin had done his rounds, announcing loudly to the world that another infidel had seen the light, the terms of the contract, the size of the marriage settlement, Allah be praised, boy! another beer.

"I hope I can take it," grinned Hardman at length. The

Tamil took his leave, his face gleaming in the sun like a polished door-knocker, strong arm raised in most cordial valediction.

Hardman started off in the direction of the car-park. Then Georges Laforgue appeared from around the corner and accosted him in French.

"It is true what I hear?"

"What do you hear, Georges?" Hardman smiled with affection and embarrassment and shame.

"You are to be married."

"Yes, Georges. I'm sorry."

"You had better come to my house. I can cook you a little lunch. Your car is here?"

Father Laforgue was a missionary who had been ten years in China, four of them in prison, a year now in Dahaga and two years yet to come before leave. He was somewhat younger than Hardman but looked far younger than he should. The fair cropped head and glasses and innocent eyes suggested a Mid-Western campus; only the mouth was mobile, adult, French. His office was displayed frankly in a long white tropical soutane that spoke of the clinic more than the altar, and the sweeping aseptic dress made sense for Hardman out of the words of *Finnegans Wake*: "He does not believe in our psychous of the Real Absence, neither miracle wheat nor soul-surgery of P. P. Quemby." Sooner or later everything in *Finnegans Wake* made sense: it was just a question of waiting.

"You're probably right," said Hardman. "If we're seen together in the street you'll probably end by being thrown out of the State. Here it is." They got into the worn dusty car, oven-like with a morning's slow soaking of metallic heat, and Hardman started it and crept, with much horning, into the stream of lunch-time bicycles and trishaws.

They clattered down Jalan Hang Tuah, turned into Jalan Rumah Jahat—chickens and children and mountainous rubbish on the road—and then, on Jalan China, came to Father Laforgue's little house. Father Laforgue lived at the end of a row of shops, all of them carrying names in bold ideograms, and he himself had his name and his calling painted on a board in white Chinese characters. Thus he became one with his Chinese parishioners, announcing a trade as honest as that of the dentist, the seller of rice-wine, the brothel-keeper, the purveyor of quack rejuvenators and aphrodisiacs, or the vendor of shark's-fin strips.

The street-door was always open, for there was nothing to steal, and Hardman was led into the single large room, dark and airless. It was dirty too, for Father Laforgue kept no servant. Once he had tried, and the Parish Committee had granted eighty dollars a month as fair wages, but lubricious eyes had suspected and tongues eventually broadcast the worst: a Chinese boy had meant pederasty, an old woman gerontophily, an intelligent monkey would have meant bestiality. It was best to do for oneself and risk the charge of auto-erotic practices. Celibacy is not merely unknown to Islam, it is unintelligible.

Hardman sat on one of the two hard chairs and saw on the table an open book which he knew to be the *Analects* of Confucius, row after falling row of ideograms preserving —outside phonetic change and above dialectal differences— that eminently seductive and dangerous common sense of old China. There were other books on the single book-shelf, all Chinese—Shang Yang, Tzu Ssu, Hui Shih, Kung-sun Lung, Chuang Chou, Han Fei, Pan Ku, Wang Ch'ung. Nowhere to be seen was the work of a new slick Thomist, Maritain, von Hügel, even Augustine or Jerome or Liguori. Georges Laforgue knew the meaning of the term 'seduction'.

Shyly the priest said, "There is nothing to drink. No, wait. I have some rice-spirit. We could drink that with altar-wine."

"That's all right, Georges."

Father Laforgue sat down, folded hands on lap, and waited.

"You knew I had to do this," said Hardman, "but it doesn't mean anything. How could it?"

"It must mean something. Why else do it?" Of the two Hardman spoke by far the better French. Diffidence smothered the knowledge of authority that rested beneath Father Laforgue's equivocal Catholicism. In China he had spoken good Mandarin, and in ten years this had become his first tongue. Here he found himself with a parish of Hokkien and Cantonese speakers and a few English people whose language he could hardly talk. His French, severed from its sources of nourishment, grown coarse through lack of use, halted and wavered, searching for the right word which Mandarin was always ready to supply. He understood the confessions he heard only because he had compiled a sort of traveller's guide to the chief sins, practising as a colonial doctor practises, the stock questions and descriptions of symptoms set out in polyglot lists to be learnt parrot-fashion.

"You know I had to get money. I'm being quite honest with you. No other way suggested itself. But, you see, it can't mean anything. I haven't apostatised; I'm just pretending to be a Muslim."

"It isn't just a question of what you believe but of what you do," said Father Laforgue. "By the mere act of going to the mosque . . ."

"But I shan't go to the mosque."

"But you will not be able to receive the sacraments, go to

mass. You'll be under Islamic law, remember. Islam is mainly custom, mainly observance. There is very little real doctrine in it, only this belief in one God, which they think so original."

"I'd thought of that, but . . ."

"And don't you see, you'll be living in sin. You'll be cohabiting with this woman, outside a state of matrimony."

"And supposing I cohabit only in the strict literal sense?"

"You mean?"

"Supposing I merely live with her, in the same house, having no carnal knowledge?"

Father Laforgue smiled, looking wise and bitter. "You know your own nature well enough. Human nature. And I think you must know the law of Islam on that point. She can claim divorce on the grounds of non-consummation. They have an Arabic term for it."

"*Nusus.*"

"I think that is the word. And then she can demand the whole of her money back, the marriage money. There is a Malay word for that."

"The *mas kahwin.*"

"Yes. You know it all."

"And you know it all."

"There was the case of a Tamil Catholic who changed his faith to marry a Malay. It was here, it happened while you were away. I was nearly thrown out of the State for trying to talk to him. I learned a lot about Islam at that time."

Hardman knew that they both knew that there was no compromise possible, no more façade, no stealing off to masses said in cellars, sacraments administered when the town was asleep, no avoiding the marriage-bed. "Look

61

here, Georges," he said. "I know what I'm doing, and what worries me most is your position. I don't want you to feel you have to try and win me back, putting yourself in bad with the Islamic authorities. You can write me off. For the time being, that is. I'll just have to take a chance. But you can't afford to go back for the lost sheep, at least your parish can't afford that you should do that."

Father Laforgue sighed. "You know my duty as far as that goes."

"It's not as though I'm a real Catholic," said Hardman. "I'm a convert, and a very recent one at that. People are always dubious about war-time marriages, and war-time conversions are sometimes just as shaky. If it hadn't been for that wing-commander having visions and this other business of the crash, well, it just wouldn't have happened."

"How do you know?"

"I'm pretty sure."

"But the fact is that it did happen. Conversions are often a matter of sheer accident. You had better have some lunch."

"I can help you."

"There is not much to do. We can have some *mee* and a little fried pork. Or are you allowed to eat that now?"

Hardman grinned. "In public, no."

"I like a man to be whole-hearted. If you are going to be a Muslim why not be a real one? It is better than being tepid. You remember it says: 'Because thou art neither hot nor cold . . .'"

"'I shall vomit thee out of my mouth.'"

"You stay there and rest. You will find some Chinese cigarettes somewhere. I will do the cooking."

Standing over the frying-pan Father Laforgue caught,

in the smell of the *mee* and the pork, the smell of the hilly province where he had lived and worked for so long. Those ten years had impaired his orthodoxy. A soldier of Rome in a far outpost, he was cut off from orders, from new policies and definitions, and had to administer the law in terms of what was expedient. The doctor, curing diseases in a savage territory, may well have to meet the medicine-man half-way and submit to the intoning of spells and the sticking of talismans between the patients' teeth before plunging his scalpel into the distempered part. And so Father Laforgue had been willing to falsify the doctrine of the Trinity in a polytheistic parish, had learned not to be outraged at meeting Chinese priests who had married. More and more he had discovered a sympathy for the charismatic churches against which St. Paul had fulmin-ated. He had held fast to his main function, primarily a thaumaturgical one: he could forgive sins, he could turn the bread and wine into God, he could save a dying child. from Limbo. Little else mattered.

And he was so sick for China that he wondered whether anything mattered now except his returning there. The Chinese Government had become more moderate recently. They would permit priests to work there now, so long as they were careful not to allow their teaching to conflict with the official philosophy. A priest, of course, was essen-tially a crying witness against the Communist metaphysic; he was nothing if he was not that. But Georges Laforgue clung to a hope. He might yet find himself back in those cool hills with their incredible stars and that mad logical world of the Chinese villagers. France meant nothing to him. Europeans had sometimes invited him to dinner and given him stuffed aubergines and onion soup and Nuits St. Georges and what they said was good coffee. They had gushed about Normandy and the Côte d'Or and little places on the Left Bank. They had played him records of French cabaret music. They had evinced, in their curious French mixed with Malay (both were foreign languages, both occupied the same compartment, they were bound to get mixed), a nostalgia for France which amused him slightly, bored him much, flattered him not at all. He rarely received invitations now to the mass-produced houses of the Public Works Department. He dined with the Chinese and spoke with the children, many of whom were learning Mandarin at school. And he had this English friend, Rupert Hardman.

"I suppose," he said, as he laid the table and put down the soya sauce, "I suppose that I am not doing things at all in the right way. I should tell you that I am the voice of the Church, which is the voice of God, and tell you to get down on your knees and repent. And then you would feel a great deal happier."

"That's perfectly true. I know I'm not going to be happy."

"And yet you do it."

"I have my function. I am a lawyer. I must fulfil that function. I cannot fulfil it with a background of debts and without an office. It's as simple as that. If you had shown me a nice rich Chinese widow it would have been easier, but . . . Well, I take what I can."

"I do not understand. You are a well-qualified man. You should be already rich. Lawyers make much money in this country."

"You can blame Redshaw and Tubb. They asked me to come and work in Singapore. They were crooks, as I found out too late. There were no repatriation terms. I had to leave, on a question of principle, and I had to stay in Malaya. There just wasn't enough money for a passage home."

"That is, I suppose, amusing. You leave your firm because of a very high principle, and now you embrace very low principles yourself."

"But that was professional honour."

"And so you set professional honour above God." Saying this, Georges Laforgue felt shame. The big words were beginning to sound empty in his mouth. Hardman had at least been seduced by honour; he himself only by hills and ridiculous impious peasants. St. Paul had been right there. Better not to have been born. But then he had been Saul. Or had he just quoted it from someone else? He ought to look that up, but he had nowhere to look it up in. He shrugged it away.

"And I shall be rich," said Hardman. "Then I shall give her all her money back. And then I shall pronounce the magic formula of divorce."

"Leaving one more divorcée abandoned to walk the streets."

"She'll never need to walk the streets."

"Right and wrong are so terribly mixed up," said Georges Laforgue. "I find it better not to think about them. I prefer to think of Confucius and human-heartedness. Now sit down and eat. I am afraid you will have to drink tepid water. I have no refrigerator."

"We shall still go on seeing each other," said Hardman. "We shall still be friends."

"Yes," said Father Laforgue, "we shall still be friends. How could we be otherwise?" He pincered into his mouth a fragment of fried pork. "But friends must meet, and it seems to me that we shall never be able to meet."

"Oh, there are places. There's the Bijou Cabaret, for

example. Police officers go there to pick up their nightly whores. We can meet there and talk philosophy, under cover of girls and beer. It will be quite easy."

"You know," said Father Laforgue, probing with his chopsticks, "my reactions are most unorthodox. I feel less hurt about your entering Islam than I would if you were to become a Protestant. That is wrong, for Protestantism is a disreputable younger brother but still of the family. Whereas Islam is the old enemy."

"The fact is," said Hardman. Waspish red peppers bit his tongue. "The fact ith that Catholithithm and Ithlam have more to thay to each other . . ." (He drank some water) ". . . than have orthodox and heterodox Christianity. It was a quarrel between men when all is said and done, and there was a healthy mutual respect. Both claimed Aristotle as master of them that know, and Dante put Averroes in a very mild place. What I mean is that you can't take Luther or Calvin or Wesley very seriously, and hence they don't count. But you can take Islam very seriously and you can compare wounds and swop photographs, and you can say: 'We're old enemies, and old enemies are more than new friends.' It's like bull-fighting and the moment of truth, when the toreador and the bull become one."

"You will come back," said Father Laforgue, nodding. "I know that. But it is important that you do not come back too late. Anyway," he added, with little conviction, "prayer may help."

"I must go back to the Law," said Hardman. "And before that I have to give some money to a parishioner of yours, a man called Hung."

"Hung is a good man."

"He's certainly wealthy enough to be able to afford to be good. And today he's going to be wealthier by two thousand dollars. More than thirty pieces of silver," he added, grinning.

"Be very careful in traffic," said Father Laforgue. "Death awaits in a pinprick. And we shall see each other soon."

"As friends."

"As friends."

When Hardman had gone, Father Laforgue, leaving the plates on the table to gather grease, turned with relief to the *Analects*. He picked out, as on a guitar-string, the notes of monosyllabic wisdom: "If a man be really bent on human-heartedness then he cannot be wicked . . ." But neither the words nor the meaning brought tears to his eyes. ". . . A wise man is not perplexed, nor is a human-hearted man unhappy, and a courageous man is never frightened." He felt hopeless at being neither wise, courageous nor human-hearted.

For Hardman the afternoon went well. The premises on Jalan Laksamana were secured, Hung counting the limp notes greedily, and Auntie's bill was paid. Then in court Hardman demolished the Chinese cook who demanded two months' pay from his ex-employer, alleging that he had not been given the statutory month's notice but had been summarily dismissed with harsh words. Hardman left the plaintiff a quivering sniveller, his treacheries and villainies open to the world, defeated and rebuked, ordered by the magistrate to pay costs at the rate of five dollars a month. Hardman's client, a paunched planter, was pleased —"Wasn't going to let that fat Chinese sod get away with it"—and he cordially invited Hardman to drink victorious whisky with him in the Club. Hardman drank quite a lot of whisky, listening to the planter's bellyaches and gripes: he was wealthy but rejected of women; even his wife, pinched, raw-boned and big-nosed, had left him for another man, a man with whom she now lived in sin in the Australian outback. Hardman was attentive and courteous, anticipating an eventual divorce suit.

When Hardman left the Club he was happy and somewhat amorous, warm images flushing his pineal gland, his marriage presented to him as an adventure, and a line from *Antony and Cleopatra* ringing clear: "The beds i' the East are soft." He drove jerkily to his fiancée's house and was met by a monsoon of abuse. 'Che Normah flashed the twin blades of her Achinese eyes and daggered him with metallic-clattering Malay. There was a lot of reduplication, and from the swirling pot of her anger he picked out *chakap-chakap* and *orang-orang Nasrani* as the main ingredients. He was accused of chatting-chatting with man-man Christian. His pale eyes glittering with whisky, he tried to take her hand, saying aloud:

"When thy mistress some rich anger shows,
Imprison her soft hand and let her rave."

She would have none of this, reiterating: "Christian men not good. Japanese Christian and Germans Christian and all bad men who have come to Malaya Christian. Christians believe in three Gods, contrary to Muslim teaching." Her Japanese girl-friend, she argued, had been Christian, and look what the Japanese had done in Malaya. And now the Chinese Communists were killing and torturing, and they too were Christian . . .

"On a point of factual accuracy," Hardman kept trying to say, "on a mere point of accuracy . . ."

Hardman was thin but he was wiry. He put his arms round her ample body and kissed her heavily. She

68

struggled in vain, only once freeing her mouth to forbid him any contact with the *padre*. Then the energy of her anger was converted to a passion of submission to his caresses, and soon, among the cushions on the floor, he anticipated the consummation of his marriage.

Convalescent, sweating, almost sober, he said: "Is it true what you told me about not being able to have children?"

"Allah has denied me that blessing."

"Are you sure it's only Allah?"

"What do you mean?"

He lay back in cigarette-smoking languor, with the silks and perfumes of the *Arabian Nights* all about him. Soon a girl would bring coffee. Minarets rose in frail spires of smoke, and the camel-bells of the robed traders thinned into the distance as the caravan passed through the gateway. It was an acceptable world.

"You must promise me that," said 'Che Normah. "Not to see that *padre* again."

"But he's my friend."

"You will have new friends."

"All right," lied Hardman. "I promise."

She embraced him with undiminished ardour and he began to feel a reluctant admiration for those Muslims who could not get along with fewer than four wives. Perhaps the West was really effete.

Next day the marriage contract was signed.

6

The thermometer in Crabbe's office read one hundred and six degrees.

It was not really the office, it was a book-store. The real office had become a class-room, housing the twelfth stream of the third standard, and soon—the *kampongs* milling out children in strict Malthusian geometrical progression —the store itself would become yet another class-room. Then Crabbe would have to take his telephone and type-writer into the lavatory. He went to the lavatory now, without typewriter or telephone, to pull off his shirt, wipe down his body with a towel already damp, and drink thirstily of the tap-water, brownish and sun-warm. For a fortnight now he had intended to buy a large thermos jug and a table-fan. His prodigious dryness was due to the heat, to too much smoking, and to a great salty breakfast.

The excessive smoking was the fault of Haji Ali College; the Pantagruelian breakfast was Ah Wing's regular notion of what an expatriate officer should eat before going off to work. Crabbe had consumed grape-fruit, iced papaya, porridge, kippers, eggs and bacon with sausages and a mutton chop, and toast and honey. At least, these things had been set before him, and Ah Wing had watched intently from the kitchen door. Crabbe now saw that he would have to beg Ah Wing to go and work for Talbot, a man who would meet his challenge gladly, might even call for second helpings and more bread. But perhaps Ah Wing would cunningly recognise Talbot's greed as pathological and despise him more than he despised Crabbe, deliberately burning his steaks and under-boiling his potatoes. Somewhere in Ah Wing's past was a frock-coated whiskered law-bringer who had established the pattern of square meals and substantial beavers. Perhaps Ah Wing was to be seen on some historical photograph of the eighteen-seventies, grinning behind a solid row of thick-limbed pioneers, all of whom had given their names to ports, hills and city streets. Certainly, in the gravy soups, turbot, hare, roast saddles, cabinet puddings, boiled eggs at tea-time and bread and butter and meat paste with the morning tray, one tasted one's own decadence: a tradition had been preserved in order to humiliate. Perhaps it really was time the British limped out of Malaya.

Ah Wing was a fantastic model of Chinese conservatism. He had not at first been willing to recognise that Crabbe was a married man and had set only one place at table. At length, grudgingly, he had obeyed his master's sign-language. And habits of long repatriated officers seemed fossilised in certain rituals: a large bottle of beer was brought to the bedside on the morning of the Sabbath; twice Ah Wing had entered Crabbe's unlocked bathroom and started to scrub his back; once Fenella had been rudely shaken from her dawn sleep and told, in rough gestures, to go.

But Ah Wing's private life—in so far as it showed chinks of light in Crabbe's kitchen-dealings with him—exhibited a much more formidable conservatism, dizzying Crabbe with vistas of ancient China. He had once caught Ah Wing eating a live mouse. A day later he was proposing to send a black cat after it (black cats were said to be tastier than tabbies). Then there was Ah Wing's store of medicines—tiger's teeth in vinegar, a large lizard in brandy, compounds of lead and horrible egg-nogs. Crabbe discovered that his cook had a great reputation with the local Malays, with whom he did a roaring trade in—eventually lethal—aphrodisiacs. The village *bomoh* was jealous of Ah Wing and called him an infidel. And indeed Ah Wing's religion, though not quite animistic, was to complex and obscure for inquiry.

The local Malays were a problem. They squatted on Crabbe's veranda every night, waiting for tales of distant lands and Western marvels. Crabbe had now established the routine of reading them love *pantuns*—mysterious four-line poems he had found in a Malay anthology—and discovered that a few verses went a long way, producing ecstatic cries, grunts of deep approval, profound nods and writhings of bodies. Here at least was a healthy literary tradition. It was Fenella who suffered most. The Malays were fascinated by her fair hair, and children were brought along to clutch it stickily, as against the King's Evil. The women asked her about her underwear, begged for discarded brassières, and went round the lounge, handling the ornaments and wanting to know how much they cost. It had taken Crabbe some time to become accustomed to Malay elders squatting on the dining-room floor and using the second bedroom for reciting their prayers. His predecessor had been decidedly too chummy. And Fenella was still scared of taking a bath, for a spirit of sincere inquiry sent serious Malay youths to the bathroom window to find out if white women differed materially from brown ones. It was not easy, and Fenella talked more and more about going back to England.

"Take it easy, darling," he would say. "We've got to be

absorbed into these customs. We're still too tough to be ingested quickly, but we've got to try and soften ourselves to a bolus, we've got to yield."

"What lovely metaphors you choose."

"I mean what I say. If we're going to live in Malaya, work for Malaya, we must shed a great deal of our Westernness. We're too ready to be shocked, and we're too reserved."

"I've tried. You know I've tried. I thought I'd succeeded in fitting into Malaya, but now I know I never shall. I've got to go home."

"But we've nothing to go back to."

"Are you so blind? Don't you see the beginning of the end already? They don't want us here. They're talking about Malaya for the Malayans. There's no room for Europeans any more."

"That's what they think. But who's to do the work if we don't? They're not ready to take over yet. In their hearts they know it."

Did they know it? Crabbe was having trouble with his senior master, Jaganathan. Jaganathan was quite sure of his own competence to take over from the white man. In the oven of an office he and Crabbe had occasionally raised their voices, and the Malay clerks had looked up with interest. Jaganathan was a black tub of a man, with a jutting rice-round belly and black trunks of legs below his white shorts. But his head was angular and carven like a huge piece of coal, polished with sweat and reflecting light in all its facets, the steel-rimmed spectacles always flashing tiny crystal moons of impatience or irritation. His middle-aged voice whined and crooned and sometimes grew husky and panting when he was deeply moved—as now, this morning, with Crabbe coming out of the lavatory, adjust-

73

ing his shirt, feeling sweat rill down the hollow of his back.

"I am telling you, Mr. Crabbe, these peoples are very angry that you will not admit their children. They are good peoples, they want to give education to their children, and they are angry that the white man will not allow them education. Then they see that two white children, the children of white men, are allowed in the school and they are not. They will be very angry to you, they will injure your car, they will throw stones at your windows."

"Look here, Mr. Jaganathan, that decision isn't mine, and you damn well know it isn't. These two expatriate officers were promised places in this school for their kids. That promise was one of the conditions of their consenting to be posted here. It was a promise made at high level, some time ago. What do you want? Do you want to deny education to the children of expatriates?"

"They should make their own arrangements for education. They have money and they should start private schools. They should not take the bread of learning from the mouths of Asians." Crabbe guessed that Jaganathan had been making a speech somewhere; the metaphor came out too glibly.

"And I wish you'd see sense about this money business," said Crabbe. "I'm sick to death of being told that I'm bloated with the blood of the down-trodden Asian. Your salary is a good deal higher than mine."

"Look at my experience. I have been teaching for many, many more years than you, Mr. Crabbe."

"Look at my qualifications," said Crabbe with heat. "Those had to be worked for, you know, and paid for. You'd better start realising that some of us are out here to work for Malaya, and that the work we do requires some sort of specialist knowledge, and that we don't regard our white skin as any qualification at all. Sometimes I wish to God I weren't white, so that I could get people to stop looking at my face as if it were either that of a leper or a jackbooted tyrant and start thinking of what I am, what I'm trying to do, not of a mere accident of pigmentation."

Jaganathan wheezed a queer chuckle which joggled his belly. "You sometimes become very angry man, Mr. Crabbe. It is not a good thing to become angry in a hot climate. The white man is not used to this climate, he is not born to it. It is better to be calm." Then his voice took on a peculiar sing-song quality, and he seemed to be soothing Crabbe, repeating the words, "Be calm, be calm, be calm," smiling and throwing the crystal lights of his glasses on to Crabbe's eyes. For a moment Crabbe had a strange conviction that Jaganathan was trying to hypnotise him. Certainly he felt spent and he tasted the fish-course of his breakfast in a wave of nausea and got a distant view, as on a radar-screen, of an approaching headache.

"All right,' 'said Crabbe. "I'm sorry." He felt a certain shame. He could not hope to help Malaya if he made enemies, lost his temper with the influential, lashed out at his henchmen. He sat down behind his desk, wiped the back of his neck with a soaked handkerchief.

"Your are not looking very well, Mr. Crabbe," said Jaganathan. "The work is very hard here. Why do you not take a little time off, lie down for a little while? There is no reason why you should not go home now."

"I'm all right," said Crabbe. "Thanks for your solicitude."

"I think perhaps you have a headache."

Crabbe looked up at him sharply. "I've no headache," he said. "Now, if you'll excuse me, I'm going to take a walk round the school. I want to see some of the teaching."

"They will not like that, Mr. Crabbe. They will resent it. They are all qualified teachers here."

"There are quite a few probationers. It's one of my jobs to see how they are getting on."

"I will come with you, Mr. Crabbe."

The headache was taking shape, firming. "Thank you, Mr. Jaganathan. I believe you yourself have a class now. If you'll excuse me." He pushed past, went out.

Crabbe got his biggest shocks from two of the experienced teachers. A shrill Tamil woman in a bright sari was giving a history lesson. Crabbe stood outside the class-room and, unseen, listened to an account of British tyranny in India.

". . . And the British hate the Indians so much they build a prison called the Black Hole of Calcutta and they put thousands of Indians in this very small dark room where there was no air and the Indians died . . ."

He gulped, wondering whether to laugh or cry, and passed on down the stone corridor to the class-room of 'Che Abdul Kadir. Kadir was evidently in the throes of a hangover and was throwing around, like stink-bombs, ripe pellets of lower deck invective.

". . . For fuck's sake, if you are going to speak this bloody language, take your finger out. Any work I give you you do not bloody well do. I stand here in great pain because I am a sick man, and I see you little bastards doing no bloody work at all grinning at me like fucking apes as if it did not matter. But . . ." He slapped the desk and contorted his Dutch-Chinese face anew. ". . . It does bloody matter. There is the future of the fucking country at stake. If you little bastards do not work then there is chaos." Suddenly his expression changed and with a sort of pedantic eagerness he wrote, in large capitals, the word

CHAOS on the blackboard. Then he stood back and looked at it, the corners of his mouth lifting in a vapid smile. "Look at that word," he said. "It is going to be an important word soon. See how it is spelt." He admired the word, licking his lips and at one point sticking out a bilious tongue. "Write it down in your books." The word seemed to cure his hangover, for he became vigorous and friendly, patting children on the back, running horny fingers through their hair, striding up and down in good humour. Meanwhile the children, looking up at each several letter with open mouths, wrote. Then Crabbe, who had been standing unseen, peering in through the glass door, entered the class-room.

"Class stand!" yelled Kadir.

Small brown faces and an occasional yellow one, wide eyes and wondering mouths. They stood and sat down again. "Look here," said Crabbe, "you can't use words like that." The children strained to hear his low voice.

"Chaos? It is not a rude word."

"No, no, I mean the other ones. 'Bastard' and 'bloody' and so on. Those aren't used in polite society." Crabbe was reasonable, affable, smiling, catching the breath of stale hops from Abdul Kadir.

"Those are common English words. All sailors in the British Navy use those words. I teach these children English as it is spoken, not from dusty books."

"Yes, yes." Crabbe was patient. "But don't you see . . ."

At the end of the long morning the headache raged and the tin of cigarettes was nearly empty. His task seemed hopeless. One young Tamil teacher had assimilated the sound-system of English so thoroughly to that of his mother-tongue that none of the Chinese and Malay children understood him. Others could not be heard beyond the first two rows. A lot of them were teaching nonsense—New York is the capital of America; Shakespeare lived in the Middle Ages; the Malays founded Singapore; "without" is a pronoun; the kidneys secrete bile. And a loose fluid arithmetic flourished in the number-melting heat, so that most answers could be marked right. Before the final bell a bright Malay boy of fourteen came in. He wanted time off to attend a "Voice of Youth" rally in Tahi Panas. The rally was to be held on a Saturday, a holiday on the West Coast but not in the strict Muslim State of Dahaga. He could travel down on the Friday, he said, and be back in time for work on the Sunday.

"But your work comes first," said Crabbe. "You can't afford to start taking time off at this stage in your career."

"This is an important meeting, sir. It is to assert the solidarity of Malay youth against the intruder."

"The intruder?"

"The non-Malays, sir. Such as the white man, sir."

"It doesn't seem a very laudable sort of thing to do. At least, it doesn't seem important enough to justify my giving you a day off."

"I can't go, sir?"

"I think it would be better if you didn't."

The Malay boy's eyes melted and his mouth drooped. "Have a heart, sir," he said. "For fuck's sake."

That night Crabbe went to the Grand Hotel to meet Hardman. Hardman had seemed shy of seeing him, and Crabbe had received no invitation to the wedding celebrations. But they had encountered each other on Jalan Laksamana in an ironmonger's shop, and Crabbe had suggested a few drinks together, finally fixing a time and a place. At the bar of the Grand, under the match-dousing fan and the cheeping house-lizards, surrounded by throat-hawkings and naked Chinese calendars, they drank beer and so warmed up the engine.

"But why did you come here?" said Crabbe.

"I might ask the same of you. Neither of us is exactly a Colonial type."

"Oh, it's a long story. My wife died."

"I thought there must be something like that. I puzzled about it quite a bit. There was that dark girl, the one who did music, wasn't there? You were always pretty thick, and I remember someone telling me during the war that you'd got married. I'm sorry."

"Oh, one gets over it. It was a ghastly business. A car smash. The damn thing went into a river. I got out all right. It was January, a very cold January. Then I married Fenella. I'd known her before: she was a post-graduate student when I was lecturing. I just couldn't get warm again. I used to shiver in bed. It was partly accident my coming here—you know, answering an advertisement when I was tight—and also a kind of helio-tropism, turning towards the heat. I just can't stand the cold."

"I can understand that. Look here, do you remember what I used to look like in the old days?"

"You were always pretty pale. I don't think you've changed much."

"You don't notice anything queer round my nose and mouth?"

"Oh, that. I thought it was a sort of peeling, sunburn or something. Isn't it?"

Hardman grinned and thrust his disfigurement into a full beer-glass. Then he said, "I had to get out because of this. Damned egotism, I suppose. It was a 'plane crash.

79

Anyway, I'd worked up such a beautiful mumbling self-consciousness about it that I became pretty useless in court. You know, like Oscar Wilde, covering my mouth up with my hand and muffling all my rhetoric. Redshaw and Tubb in Singapore wanted somebody to join them, so I came out. My point was, I suppose, that all white men here are white to the same degree, and people—Asians, I mean—would stare anyway. So what the hell. Look, let's have some whisky."

"Yes. Whisky. And now you're married."

"Now I'm married. I'm sorry I didn't invite you to the reception."

"As you said. Did you have the usual Malay business —you in uniform and kris, recalling the glories of ancient Malacca, and the medicine-man's mumbo-jumbo?"

"You don't have that when one of you's been married before. Just a contract and then orange crush for the mosque officials and then alcohol for the rest of the boys. It strikes me I'm a better Muslim than most of them. God, what a night. Abdul Kadir . . ."

"Yes. For fuck's sake."

"Oh, they're all right. They're a bit more alive than the Club boys."

"And the wife?"

"You know, she's pretty good." Hardman drank some whisky and water. "I think it's going to work out all right. Mind you, Malay women are pretty demanding."

"So I've heard." Crabbe opened his mouth to speak of Rahimah, then shut it again. She obviously still meant something to him.

"It's not lasciviousness, not really. It's a means of checking whether you've been with another woman."

On that cue-line Mrs. Talbot entered. She swung open

the bar-door and stood glaring, her eyes a little out of focus, her lipstick smeary, dishevelled. She was wearing a smart crisp cocktail dress, patterned with lozenges of local silver thread. She had evidently been drinking. She said:

"Where is he?"

"Who?" said Crabbe politely, coldly, standing.

"You know damn well. Bannon-Fraser. He's upstairs, isn't he?"

"Madam," said Hardman, "I've just no idea." At a single table a couple of Chinese drinkers looked up incuriously. Then Auntie appeared, huge, with great welcoming arms. "Ah," she said, "this is great pleasure. You do not honour us as often as you should."

"Is Mr. Bannon-Fraser upstairs?"

"Mr. Bannon-Fraser is not here, not to-night."

"He's upstairs, with that bitch."

"He is with no bitch, at least here he is not. Elsewhere he may be."

"I'm going up to look." Mrs. Talbot made towards the main room.

"That is private," said Auntie. "That is for residents." Her bulk barred the way. "You come over here to the bar and have a little drink. With me." She steered Mrs. Talbot across, her beef-red ham-hand on the fragile arm. Mrs. Talbot flopped on to a bar-stool, elbows on the counter, then started to snivel. "All alike," she sniffed. "You're all alike." Then she turned on Hardman viciously. "You with your bloody Catholic virtue," she said. "Not too virtuous to . . ."

"All right." Hardman snapped it out. "Not here."

"What's it going to be, my dear?" said Auntie ingratiatingly. "Gin?"

"Double whisky."

"Look here," said Hardman to Crabbe, "I've got to go. I promised to be back by ten." He winked and jerked his head in the direction of Mrs. Talbot's back, bowed over the bar. "Drop in at the office sometime."

"I'm going myself," said Crabbe. Then he looked at Mrs. Talbot, wife of the State Education Officer, getting drunk, not herself, alone, not fit to drive. "In a minute or so," he added. Hardman winked again and went out quietly. Auntie waved, winking, conspiratorial.

"It is so nice to see you here," said Auntie to Mrs. Talbot. "It would be nice to see you more often. Sometimes we have parties, with nice people from Bangkok and Penang. They like to meet nice European people."

"Oh God, God," said Mrs. Talbot. "I don't want to meet anyone ever again." She drained her whisky and called "Boy!"

"Look here," said Crabbe, "have a tomato juice. Chilled. Have you eaten anything?"

She laughed without mirth. "There's always eating in our house. Non-stop performance. For God's sake don't mention food to me."

"Don't have any more whisky," said Crabbe. "Please."

She lolled her head at him. "You trying to protect me from the worse side of my nature or something?" She lisped slightly, little-girlish, looking at him still while drinking whisky steadily from the full glass.

"Let me take you home," said Crabbe.

"You think I'm not fit to drive or something?" It was the same high child's voice of innocence.

"Come on, let me take you home. He'll be worried about you."

"Who? Bannon-Fraser? He'll be worried when I see him." The voice had modulated to full woman. "I'll

82

give him something to worry about. The swine. The worm."

"We have nice people coming here," said Auntie. "There is a radiogram. There can be dancing."

"You can leave your car here," said Crabbe. "A boy can bring it along in the morning. Come on, let me take you home."

"You keep harping on that." The little-girl coquette. "You got designs on me? Oo, how exciting."

"And there is a new cook," said Auntie. "Chinese. He is paid a hundred and fifty a month."

"One for the road," said Mrs. Talbot, "before Mr. Crabbe takes me to my lonely bed. Or his lonely bed. Which?" She goggled at him, swaying, some scum at the corners of her mouth.

"Come on," said Crabbe, taking her arm.

Outside it was drizzling. Mrs. Talbot lost her balance, fell to the wall. "Steady," said Crabbe. He put an arm round her. "My car's here, round the corner."

The Abelard stood, smooth and ghostly in the faint street lighting. It was evident that nobody would get home in it, not that night. All the tyres were slashed. Mr. Jaganathan's good peoples, their vicarious thirst for learning thwarted by the wicked white man, had presumably sipped a small revenge. Crabbe, holding up Mrs. Talbot, swore.

"Look what the swine have done to my tyres."

Mrs. Tallbot saw the joke. She laughed full-throatedly, almost soberly. "It's not at all funny," said Crabbe.

"Now you'll have to come home with me," she said.

"Give me your ignition-key."

"No. I drive my own car."

"You can't, not to-night. Give me that key."

"No. Get inside."

Crabbe hesitated. She seemed somewhat more sober. Her speech was not slurred. She fitted the ignition-key into the switch deftly.

"Well. Are you coming?

She drove too fast but her reactions were normal enough. She darted from side to side of the road but was quick with her brakes. A home-going trishaw driver missed death by many yards.

"Look," said Crabbe, "this isn't the way." She had branched off the main road and was speeding towards the airport. She paid no attention. "This isn't the way," he repeated.

"No, dear. I know it isn't the way."

"Then what the hell are you doing?"

"Don't you know, dear? There's a nice quiet spot up this road where you and I can be rather cosy."

"But, damn it all . . ."

"Just what I say. Damn it all. And *them* all. You're only young once."

Physical pleasure is in itself a good, and some mystics say that God is good precisely as the taste of an apple is good. Anyway, one should not withdraw from the proffered good, despite morality, honour, personal pride (having her revenge on Bannon-Fraser), the knowledge that sooner or later there will be a hell of a row. Crabbe took what he was offered, as one would take slices of orange or a peeled banana. Meanwhile the drizzle rattled on the car-roof and the red light of the control-tower glowed—in vain.

7

"Brother, brother! Do not be forever in your shop. Come today and drink with us."

Mohinder Singh hesitated. It was all very well for *them*. Kartar Singh was a police constable, fat and happy in the realisation that even now, two years before retirement, he would not gain promotion. Teja Singh was a deep sigh of rock-bottom insouciance, night-watchman outside a Chinese hotel. Neither had anything to lose. He, Mohinder Singh, had his way to make, a great deal to lose, the big sale of the year to miss on a random wanton day off. He hesitated.

Kartar Singh was so fat as to generate in the beholder a re-orientation of æsthetic standards. His was a fatness too great to be gross, a triumphant fatness somehow admirable, an affirmative pæan, not a dirge of wasted muscle and over-indulged guts. This fatness *was* Kartar Singh: it was the flesh singing, in bulging cantilenas and plump pedal-notes, a congenital and contented stupidity, a stupidity itself as positive as the sun. A mere week before, Kartar Singh had been patrolling the streets with a younger constable—a keen Malay boy—and the clock above the bank had struck the hour. "We are finished now," said the boy. "It is time for us to report off duty at the station." "How do you know?" said Kartar Singh. "The clock has just struck," said the Malay. Kartar Singh laughed heartily and said, "Don't be silly, that is nothing. The clock is always making that noise."

Teja Singh was all dirty grey hair and straggling piebald beard, dirty whites and a turban that always needed adjusting. He slept all night on his watchman's bed and he slept off his sleep during the day. Now he was taking a rare holiday from sleep.

"See," said Kartar Singh. "Here is a bottle of good *samsu* I have received as a bribe from a Chinese. It is a very light colour. That shows it is good. Take money from your till, brother, for we have none, and let us go to some *kedai* for a day's merrymaking."

Mohinder Singh hesitated. He looked round his shop—the rolls of cloth, the soapstone elephants, the underpants, the dummy teats, the razor-blades, the single camphor-wood chest and said, "It is difficult. A shopkeeper should keep to his shop."

"Not always, brother. We Sikhs must have our occasional meetings. We are so few, and the other races are so many. We must show a solid face to the world, show that we are one. Come, brother, dip your hand in that overflowing till and accompany to us some *kedai* for a day's merrymaking."

Mohinder Singh took from the till all that it contained—two dollar notes and a handful of small change—and locked his shop door. He glanced suspiciously at the withered Chinese who sat in underpants, picking his teeth, outside the druggist's shop next door, and also at the Malay tailor on the other side. "I should not be doing this," he said; "the rent has not been paid this month."

"What is rent, brother? It is the tyranny of landlords. Let us go."

Arm in arm they proceeded along the covered five-foot

way, greeting various acquaintances. They entered Cheng Leong's Muslim Eating Shop, took a central table, and called loudly for glasses. Then they uncorked their *samsu* and drank to each other.

"What is to become of us," asked Teja Singh, "when they have their independence? I see bad times ahead for Sikhs."

"The Sikhs against the world," said Kartar Singh. "What are a few Malays and a few more Chinese? We are a warrior race, we can fight for our rights."

"Where is your bangle?" asked Mohinder Singh. "You are not wearing the bangle on your wrist. A Sikh should not be without his bangle."

"I found a way of using it to open beer bottles, brother. By ill luck it broke. But I shall get another one."

"We have been pushed around," said Teja Singh. "We are human beings, like any other people living in the world. But where will you see your wealthy Sikhs, or your Sikhs in their offices with many telephones and riding in their big cars? I say the Sikhs have been cheated, and when this independence comes they will be cheated even more."

Two Malay workmen entered, old dish-towels round their heads. They had been pounding the road and were tired. They wanted two glasses of iced water. One looked at the huge belly of Kartar Singh with contempt and said to his colleague:

"There they are, the fat sods. Bearded prawns, my father used to call them. They carry shit in their heads just like prawns, he used to say."

"Fat at our expense. No work to do. Drinking the day away. Sucking the marrow from the bones of the Malays."

"Right. But things are going to be different soon. Sikhs and Chinese and Tamils and white men . . . Did you hear of that new white man who runs the school?"

"No."

"He has a wife with gold hair, but he spent the whole night at that fat white woman's hotel, sleeping with another woman. His car was outside all night. When the fathers and mothers of some of the school-children found out they slashed his tyres."

"Ah."

"And he was with another white woman in a car just by the flying-ship place. Half the night, they say. That's what things are coming to. Godlessness and sleeping with women. And such men are to teach in the schools. But things are going to be different soon."

"There is a white man who has married a Malay woman and has entered the Faith. You have heard that? He is a very white man."

"Entered the Faith. They pretend to enter the Faith to marry our girls. And then when they go home it is all finished. I have heard too many such stories. And this man certainly has a wife in his own country. They are a treacherous lot."

"There will be a reckoning soon."

"Yes. Call for two more glasses of cold water."

The *samsu* was going down well. Mohinder Singh said, "No one can deny that at least one Sikh has shown enterprise. There are very few in trade. But, please God, I shall yet have a car and assistants and a telephone. And then you will be proud of me."

"We all show enterprise," said Kartar Singh. "It requires enterprise to be a good policeman. And perhaps," he added, "to be a good night-watchman. The Sikhs are everywhere engaged in the important things. Guarding the lives of those who are sleeping, guarding valuable property, tending cattle so that there shall be fresh milk, and in the

88

post offices and on the railway stations you will find them. They are the backbone of this country."

"We will drink to the Sikhs," said Mohinder Singh.

One of the Malay workmen belched briefly on a gulp of cold water. The Sikhs looked across, dark fiery eyes over warriors' beards, the ghostly swords of their ancestors at the ready. "Ignore them," said Teja Singh.

The bottle went round and round, and turbans were cocked awry. A Chinese came in for a cup of coffee, a harmless youth who was a clerk in the Airways office. He smoked a cigarette over a newspaper.

"There he is," said one of the Malay workmen. "A pincered crab. Smoking his cigarette like a bloody raja and pretending to read that paper. It stands to reason you can't write down words that way. Like kids' drawings."

"Their time is coming," said the other. "There won't be a Chinese alive when we get independence."

"Another glass of water. Then we'd better get back to work."

Customers came and went, but the Sikhs stayed. They became happier and happier, the potent lead-poison of *samsu* heartening them, crying great music through their arteries. Soon Kartar Singh obliged with a song:

> "A bird sat high on a banyan tree,
> Carolling night and carolling day,
> And on the heads of the passers-by . . ."

"Look," said Teja Singh, "we have no more *samsu*. And we have spent Mohinder Singh's money on nuts."

"We will sell something," said Mohinder Singh recklessly. "We will sell something from the shop. Better, we

89

will take the camphorwood chest to the pawnbroker's. He
will lend us good money on it."

> "And each bemerded passer-by
> Cried loud in anger on that bird
> Carolling night and carolling day,
> Wiping from his eye . . ."

"A third at least of its value," cried Mohinder Singh.
"One cannot work all the time. Even the self-employed
man is entitled to his relaxation. We will go now."

"I must go to work at ten o'clock," said Teja Singh. "The
watchmen of the shops are less lucky. They seek their
watchman's bed at six. I have greater responsibilities and
must not abuse them."

"We shall not be late. See, the sun is but setting. There
is time enough."

> "And still that bird upon the tree,
> Carolling night and carolling day,
> Ignored the plaints of the passers-by . . ."

But, sitting by the opening of Ismail's Muslim Eating
Shop, Inder Singh was spooning in soup, tall, thin,
saturnine, his beard cut, contrary to the laws of religion,
trimmed in a Mephistophelian manner, his turban neat
and starched, so that it could be doffed and donned like a
skullcap. He was midway between the old Sikh and the
new—bald and smoking—and read the modern books of
the West. He was a teacher at the Haji Ali College. He
greeted his co-religionists and offered them beer.

> "Let us like birds upon the tree,
> Carolling night and carolling day,

Ignore each hairless passer-by,
And say . . ."

"And how is the white man there?" asked Teja Singh,
politely.

"As the rest," said Inder Singh. "He has much to learn.
He sweats too much. His shirt is like cellophane at all
hours of the morning."

"And his wife, the gold-haired one?" asked Mohinder
Singh. "She flew with me that time, she and I, from
Timah."

"She grows thin and never smiles."

"Ah."

They drank and laughed full-beardedly, rolling in their
chairs. The *kedai* had a tame bird which hopped from
table to table, chirping and pecking rice-grains. This they
petted, calling it pet-names, accusing it of being a spy, of
being able to fly back to their wives and tell tales of their
spendthrift bibulosity. They had a very good time.

"Now I must go home to my wife," said Kartar Singh.
"About now she expects me."

There were great obscene jokes about strongly-made beds
and convenient positions. In high spirits, Kartar Singh
told the story about the man who took the wrong bottle
of urine to the Medical Officer. It was a very good evening.

Down Jalan Laksamana they staggered. Next to
Mohinder Singh's shop the Chinese druggist still sat, reading a newspaper in the neon-light, a toothpick fixed in his
mouth. He looked up at Mohinder Singh staggering, arms
round his friends, and rebuked him in staccato Chinese
Malay.

"Early this evening," he said, "a red-haired dog came, a
woman with gold hair. She wanted to buy many things

91

from your shop. She wanted a camphorwood chest . . ."

"No!"

"And many yards of silk. And also a comb. And glasses and tea-cups. And also mattresses . . ."

"No!"

It was not all lies. He was right about the comb.

"This may be as a warning. If you are to do trade you must do trade. It is not right for a shop-man to go roistering off . . ."

"Why did you not call me? You know where I was. . . ."

"And leave my shop? It is the first rule of trade—always to be there. There is only one man on this street who is not always there, except for you, Sikh. He is the white lawyer. He too has no trade sense. But if you wish to learn the hard way . . ."

Mohinder Singh turned on his fat friend and gave him a feeble punch in the belly. The old Chinese cackled with pleasure.

"You come seducing me from the right way, spending money from the till. How shall I succeed like this? Now you give me the trouble of going up to the white woman's house with the things she wishes to buy. And there is the cost of a taxi, of two taxis. You are no true friend. . . ."

"You will not hit me in the belly like that. I tell you, men have died for less. If you dare to do that again . . ."

"It is not right," said Teja Singh, "to hit him again off his guard. He was not expecting that. . . ."

"You are a false friend. Now I am ruined. Now my honour is besmirched."

A little crowd had collected, including two Malay workmen with towels round their heads. One said to the other:

"Hairy sods. When they're not drinking they're fighting."

"More money than sense," said his friend. "Shit in their heads."

"Like prawns."

"Like prawns."

The Sikhs had grown heated. Angry words flew. Soon Kartar Singh cried:

"If you continue to abuse me, I shall call the police." The word started something off in his slow mind. "Police. By God, I am the police." He sought in his pocket for a whistle.

"Ruined. . . . Moreover . . ."

"And it is certainly no friendly act . . ."

"And when you come to consider it soberly . . ."

"If you dare to do that again . . ."

"Apart from that . . ."

Crabbe and Fenella drove past, on their way to the party at the Istana. "Look," said Fenella, "it's beginning. Riots, fights, brawls. Tomorrow it will be murders. Oh, let's go home, Victor. Let's go home."

"Quiet, dear," said Crabbe. "Do please be quiet."

8

"Look," said Crabbe, warm orange crush in his hand, "I'm not starting anything."

"Oh, you make me sick." Anne Talbot looked demurely ravishing, as was her intention, in a very low-cut evening frock of bottle-green, choker of Kelantan silver, ear-rings in the shape of small sharp *krises*. She was painted, white-washed, rouged, scented, heady, intimidating, goddess-like, irresistible, like any other personable woman in evening dress, more especially here where the flash-point was low, under a tropic moon, among palms, orchids, hibiscus, brown polished bodies. "Sick, sick, sick."

"And I didn't start anything," said Crabbe, "as you know." He was sweating into his white tuxedo, his shirt dark with wet, feeling heavy, lumpish, boorish, the orange crush in his hand growing warmer and more undrinkable.

"It isn't a question of who starts," said Anne Talbot. "It's all a question of what starts. Look," she added, "that Asian over there, the one in glasses, is pouring something into the glass of that other man, the one with a turban and a moustache. I'm sure it's gin. Do go and see if you can get some. Here, take my glass."

"Yes," said Crabbe. "Kadir and Haji Zainal Abidin. But I'm not starting anything."

At the flood-lighted end of the Great Hall, under high gilt beams, the Sultan sat on his throne, Yang Maha Mulia

Sultan Idris ibni Al-Marhum Sultan Yassin, smiling somewhat foolishly as though drugged for the occasion, the occasion of his sixty-third birthday. Smoke rose high—cigarettes and golden table-lighters brought round by undeferential white-coated flunkeys—but there was nothing to drink except orange crush—officially. In the lavatories, behind screens, pillars, out among the bushes, flasks and bottles flashed amid giggles and guffaws, and improvident newcomers to the State grew sour in sight of the hilarity of the long-seasoned.

The Abang, God bless his name, was talking to Fenella. He wore Malay evening dress of rich tunic, trousers and apron, his well-shaped head sleek under a velvet *songkok*. He was a handsome man, his face a fine blend of Bugis and Siamese, his hair black and thick at fifty, his moustache luxuriant, shaking the confining bars of its recent neat clipping. He spoke English well, using it efficiently like any other tool of government, but unseduced by the connotations of its words. He had been taught it by a Japanese, alumnus of an American university, and nothing could have better emphasised his independence of the fussy British arm of protection than those drawled sound-track vowels and brash folky idioms. He was talking to Fenella because he proposed, at leisure, to attempt her seduction. There was no question of personal attraction: it was a tradition among his ancestors that power had been granted to the family by the fair-haired Ghost Princess and that the blood of the family must be refreshed whenever possible by copulation with blonde women. He now attempted to make a preliminary appointment with her—lunch at the Istana—in the hallowed language of film.

"You're kind of pretty. Pretty as a picture. I guess they all tell you that."

"Really . . ." Fenella looked well in black, her skin faintly flushed with sun, the rich gold in tight curls above her tiny ears.

"I reckon you and me could get together. We could meet some place and talk. We could have a real long talk and get kind of better acquainted."

"My husband . . ."

"I guess I haven't had the pleasure of making his acquaintance. I understand he's a very lovely person, though. They tell me he's making a real fine job of the College."

"I mean, I don't want to seem rude or anything . . ."

"I guess he'll be understanding. He won't think you're rude or anything. How's about lunch tomorrow?"

Rupert Hardman slunk about self-consciously in a *songkok*. His wife, magnificent in a tight European gown, had insisted that he wear this token of his conversion, and after a quarrel in which he had seen, perhaps for the first time, the potential heat of her temper, he had submitted with an ill grace. He felt foolish under the black oval cap and he sought strong drink from Abdul Kadir. Haji Zainal Abidin greeted Hardman with loud harsh laughter and a vista of red throat and many teeth. He cried:

"Tonight they try to make us both bloody fools, me in my *haji's* turban and you in that stupid little cap. Still," he said, gulping orange crush that was fat with gin, "we must proclaim to the world that we are of the Faith. Not like this bloody fool here who looks like a bloody tramp."

Abdul Kadir had come straight from a party in one of the town *kedais*, and had had little time to change. He had borrowed a pair of white trousers too small for him, and his shirt, lacking collar-buttons, gaped at the throat, disdaining the weak constriction of a loosely knotted tie.

96

He blinked nervously over his glasses, trying to hide in a huge hairy hand his flask of gin. Soon, Hardman foresaw, he would grow nautical, jolly Jack in port for the night, cursing and blinding but, like a court jester, without rebuke.

"For fuck's sake," said Kadir. "What kind of a fucking party is this, anyway?" Hardman took his slug of gin and moved off to talk to the fat young Protector of Aborigines. The exposition of Kadir's nocturnal symphony was beginning.

"False pretences," said the fat young Protector of Aborigines. "Everything is granted under false pretences in this damn place." He poured orange crush into his lively greasy face, and said: "I understood this was a straightforward anthropological job. But, damn it all, it's political —trying to get the aborigines on the right side, bribing them with nicotine to accept the democratic faith. And I can't learn the language. Nobody's ever thought of giving it an alphabet, and I'm essentially a visual type. In Africa they put me in a native hut for six months, made me live with a family, just to learn the language. It was no damned good."

"No?"

"After six months all I could do was point at things— that's what my hosts did—and when I got back to Nairobi I found I was making unequivocal gestures at the women in the Club, and that didn't go down at all well." He sighed. "I find anthropology much more attractive in a library. Sir James Frazer did a lot of harm really, making the whole thing so Hellenic and aseptic. I don't think I'm really cut out for field work."

"But it is important," said Mr. Jaganathan, polished and round in his white dinner jacket, "that you do your best to combat Communism in these primitive communities. It is insidious ideology." Mr. Jaganathan had again been making a speech somewhere.

"Oh, we talk too much about ideology," said Hardman. "When people are only concerned with ideology it's harmless enough, a kind of intellectual game, one that we all played when we were undergraduates. In the late thirties and early forties it was very popular, but it didn't tie up in any way with machine-guns and barricades and gaschambers. It was, to use our friend's term, Hellenic and aseptic."

"I am shocked to hear these things," said Mr. Jaganathan, a great gush of insincerity coming from his inclined left armpit. "For here the British always prided themselves on bringing the justice and the institutions of their traditional parliamentary democracy. And they who came here were always the kind of persons you mention — good clever young men from the universities."

"It doesn't last," said Hardman. "Why, look at your boss over there: Conservative, Christian, almost reactionary." He gestured towards Crabbe, who was delivering a long frowning speech to Mrs. Talbot. "He was a great Communist when I knew him, leader of the Communist Group and all that sort of thing. His conversation was thick with Lenin. But he changed."

"That is very interesting what you tell me," said Mr. Jaganathan. "I did not know Mr. Crabbe was a Communist." He drank to his discovery.

"You are very kind," said Fenella to the Abang. "I must see if I can persuade my husband to let me come." She looked for her husband and found Anne Talbot simpering at him in a far corner. "But I don't think he will mind."

"That's swell," said the Abang. "I'll send a car round

for you. Would you like to see my cars? I've got a swell collection, finest in the Federation, every kind you can think of."

"We have an Abelard," said Fenella.

"An Abelard? That's one kind I don't have. You don't see many in these parts. An Abelard. Well . . ." He began to steer Fenella to the royal garages at the back of the Istana.

"I don't think I'd better," said Fenella. "People are looking."

"Of course they're looking. It isn't often they see a dame like you."

To the sound of a bugle, covers were whisked off the buffet tables that were ranged on each side of the long hall. Plates of cold meat were disclosed, rolls, platters of rice and brown viscous curry. There was a rush, headed by Talbot.

Crabbe found himself set upon by starving rajas who stabbed forks into his hand. They stabbed indiscriminately —here a slice of dried-up beef, there a chicken-wing, here a dripping hunk of cold curried mutton, there a human hand. Talbot fought his way out, protesting loudly, holding his spoils clear of the stabbing. From the dark recesses of the hall odd dark men had appeared, the scavengers. Crabbe observed a tall intellectual-looking Indian in a creased suit; he was cramming his pockets with meat passed to him by a tiny raja. Crabbe was interested to note that the flunkeys joined in with the guests, laughingly grabbing ice-cream and dishes of pickle, and that rank was forgotten in this elemental clawing for food. Every man for himself, including the Abang. The essential Malaya is jungle.

After refreshments came dancing. The sole dance band

of Dahaga sat in the musicians' gallery, discoursing approximate versions of popular tunes, in unison and without bar-lines. Cars went and came, bearing more gin and whisky. The brightly coloured wrapper of orange crush passed around, the dry bread of delectable hilarious sandwiches.

"Would it interest you to know," whispered Anne Talbot, all close mobile perfume and softness and warmth, "that I love you?"

"Even if it were true," said Crabbe, "it wouldn't elate me, it would worry me. God knows I've enough trouble." He muffed a reverse turn. "Sorry."

"But it's true," said Anne Talbot. "Why don't you hold me closer? Fenella's not looking. She's otherwise occupied."

Fenella sat with the Abang.

"Oh, Anne," said Crabbe, "for God's sake don't start anything."

"You can always fabricate a conference in Kuala Lumpur. And I can always visit a friend in Singapore."

"No. Please, no."

"No," said the Secretary of the State War Executive Committee, a ginger man with a Lancashire accent, "it's not finished yet, not by any means. And won't be for a long time."

"I'm sorry to hear that," said Hardman.

"Ruperet," came a shrill voice from the dance-floor, "put on your *songkok*."

"These political boys want to think it's over. It's one way of getting us out, see. But they're still there in the jungle, and we can't get at them. There's a screen of aborigines all round them, and they're getting food and weapons and doing fine. And then these independence boys accuse us of faking things. Do you know, we brought them a couple of packs and rifles and even a cap with a star on it—genuine stuff, captured in the jungle—and they said, bold as brass, that we'd bought it at Whiteaway's."

"Too bad."

"But there's food getting through. God knows how, but it's getting through. The rice ration's down to nearly damn-all in the *kampongs*, but we keep finding dumps of grub in the jungles. We're worried to death and you'd think we'd get a bit of sympathy. Damn it all, it's their country, not ours . . ."

"For fuck's sake, take your fucking hands off me."

"Come on, Kadir, like a good boy. We'll get some nice black coffee down the road."

"I'm not fucking drunk."

"Nobody said you were. A bit tired, that's all. It's been a long day."

"Don't fucking touch me."

"Come on now. Grab his other arm, Kassim."

"We could have such a good time in K.L. There's a nice little hotel where nobody ever goes."

"I guess you're always being told you're beautiful. I won't say what the other guys say. I'll just say that you look like something special to me."

"I was given a special piece of information to-night. Our Mr. Crabbe is known to have been prominent Communist."

"No."

"Yes. But then I say always that beneath every Christian you will find Communist leanings. It is the same sort of faith. But Hindus are always good peoples. We have too many gods to become Communist."

"Yes."

"But this is to be thought about seriously. It is terrible that the College should be run by prominent Communist."

"Terrible."

At midnight the party ended. The Sultan was bowed off to his quarters, to the accompaniment of a sketchy version of the State anthem, and the guests sought their cars. At the portals of the Istana the Abang met Crabbe for the first time. He shook his hand warmly, his eyes bright with pity, for Crabbe was doubly to suffer: he was to be robbed of his car, he was to be cuckolded.

Crabbe and Fenella drove home sulkily. As they neared the *kampong*, one said to the other:

"I didn't see much of you this evening."

"Nor I of you."

"What was going on anyway?"

"Exactly. What was going on?"

"I was just being sociable."

"One can take sociability too far. Everybody was looking at the pair of you."

"Everybody was looking at the pair of *you*."

"Oh, well, it doesn't matter."

"No. I don't suppose anything matters."

Crabbe slept fitfully that night, the moon on his face, the China Sea in his ears. At four in the morning he awoke, sweating and terrified by the old dream, dream of a ghost he had thought exorcised for good. He was with his first wife in the car on the freezing January road. The skid, the crashed fence, the dive of the whirring car to the icy water of the river, the bubbling, the still body in the passenger-seat, the frantic ascent through fathoms of lead to the cold breath of the living night, the crime which could not be expiated.

He sat up in bed and smoked a cigarette. The faint noises were attributes of night's silence—the small clicks of the hunting house-lizards, the power-house drone of the refrigerator, the distant frog-croaks, Fenella's steady breathing. He looked at her still shape on the neighbour bed, and felt pity. She had given so much to him but could never receive in return the warmth he bestowed even on a casual mistress. It could not be helped: there was just nobody to take the place of the first, the only. And yet he had thought there was a chance, especially when his fear of driving a car again had been banished by another fear—that time when Alladad Khan had been shot in the arm by the ambushing terrorists and there had been nothing for it but to seize the steering-wheel. But the dream had come back and a sinking realisation that Fenella was not to him what she should be, and hearing the sea's beating now he shuddered at the thought of water closing over his head again, of his being enclosed by the element of another woman.

He got up, unable to seek sleep again, frightened of re-entering that dream again, and left the bedroom. In the lounge he poured himself some whisky and sipped it very slowly. On the table, he noticed, was a poem that Fenella had started. The manuscript was much scarred with fastidious alterations, searchings for the right word and rhythm. He read it, pitying.

Land where the birds have no song, the flowers
   No scent, and time no movement; here
The rhythms of northern earth are frozen, the hours
   Set like ice-cubes; the running of the year

Is stopped and comma'd only by the moon's feasts,
    And the sun is Allah, never an avatar;
In sight of that constant eye life crumbles, wastes
To the contented champing patterns of the beasts
    Which live in day's denomination. Far

The life of years and works that yet a day's
    Flight can restore . . .

It was not a very good poem—confused, the rhythms
crude. Poor Fenella. But the fact of her unhappiness was
very much to be taken into account, and certainly she
would never be happy here in the East. It was not her
fault. She belonged to the North, the world of spring and
autumn and the cultures that spring out of a weakening
and strengthening sun—winter sables over bare shoulders
that would glow in central heating, books by the fire and
myths out of the fire. She wanted to go home, but not
without him. Twice he had suggested that she go back to
London, to wait till the end of the tour and long leave
together. But what after that? He proposed to come back,
work for Malaya till retirement, or for as long as Malaya
would let him. And, unable to give her much love, he at
least should give her part of what she wanted—to be with
him, living somewhere where she could have her libraries
and music and ballet and conversation about art, for it did
not matter much to him where he lived. Except that he
felt his place now was in Malaya, his duty to show Malaya
those aspects of the West which were not wholly evil, to
prepare Malaya for the taking over of the dangerous
Western engine.

He went back to bed and dozed till the dawn came—the
mass-produced invariable tropical dawn, greeted by no

bird-chorus, a dawn assignable to all months in this land of no seasons. The *kampong* folk would now be eating cold rice and the fishermen would be tramping down to the beach. And in the kitchen Ah Wing would happily be putting the kettle on and gathering the materials for another gargantuan breakfast. She was right about the day's denomination, the single cubes of time—the porridge, then the kippers, then the bacon and eggs, then the routine of work: the champing pattern of the beast that occasionally looked up at the moon. Right or wrong, it was his way; since that January night he had lost the desire for more complex and civilised patterns.

9

The Abang, of course, was aware that his days were numbered. He did not repine. He and his forebears had had their fill of power, possessions, women. Money was salted away in Australia, there were rubber and tin shares, a fleet of cars, jewels, precious stones, heirlooms of all kinds. Whatever happened, the Abang and his numerous progeny would never starve. It might be necessary for him to spend a glamorous exile in Cannes or Monaco or Capri, places which he had not yet seen, but he had a rough idea of what the West was like, and he had visions of new kinds of power, perhaps being lifted—like certain other royal sons of the Prophet—to heights of Occidental myth through marriage with Hollywood film-stars. He saw himself, in a smart suit and a *songkok,* bowed into the opulent suites of Ritzes and Waldorfs and baring, under dark glasses, a hairy chest to a milder sun by a snakeless sea. He saw himself entering the Casino, he heard the hush of respect for exiled royalty.

Royalty. There was the joke, of course. There was not a drop of royal blood in his well-set randy body. Meanwhile, there were true rajas picking up a few dollars a month as school-teachers, *tengkus* working in shops. Back in the misty reaches of the annals of Dahaga—part history, part legend—some vigorous peasant had obtained a hold over a sultan senile or insane with tertiary syphilis, and the myth had come into being. He himself did not believe in the story of the descent from the fæces of a sacred bull, or in the magical accolade of the Ghost Princess, but he accepted the power of a tradition which could raise earth-red blood above that watery blue which ran in some of the lowliest channels of the State. The rajas and the *tengkus* bowed with joined hands to one whose very title was a rough *kampong* shout, for 'Abang' was the name one called contemptuously at boy-servants whose real names one did not know. *Abang* meant 'elder brother'.

The Abang had read George Orwell and was struck by the exquisite appropriateness of the title of the Ruler of Oceania. It had amused him for a time to consider sticking posters throughout Dahaga, posters bearing, below the image of his own powerful head, the legend: *SI-ABANG MEMANDANG AWAK*. But it was doubtful if his Malay subjects would have seen the point. All right, he was watching them. Why was he watching them? Did he admire their beauty, or something? If he was watching them, they could equally well be watching him. Where was all this watching getting anyone? What was there to watch, anyway? But, of course, all his subjects were proles.

The rule of the Abang, in an age when the techniques existed to lapidify any rule to permanency, was, because of the very rise of a party, doomed. There was this new thing, politics; there were these cries of *Merdeka!* A new class was arising—small intellectuals, failed B.A.s, frustrated lawyers, teachers with the gift of the gab. Another year, and there would be independence. Sultans would be in an anomalous position, and Abangs would be in no position at all. Centralisation, directives, much paper, a spectacled bureaucracy, but this time not a haughty white face to be seen anywhere in the air-conditioned offices. The British would be pulling out soon and, with them, the last of the feudal rulers.

It was, in a sense, curious that the end of colonialism meant also the end of a grotesque seigniory in Dahaga. In another sense, it was not. The British were much given to anomalies—anomalies of character, anomalous ethics, constitutional anomalies. But there would be no anomalies in the new régime: there would be a bright white light to sweep away the romantic, Gothic shadows. And then, if the dynamo failed, another dynamo would be imported and there would be a bright red light. There was going to be a dream of order—perhaps, thought the Abang, itself a kind of romanticism, but a romanticism dangerous because self-deceptive—based on a racial mystique, most probably. But the Abang feared the red hordes whose advance parties crouched in the jungle. They had no dream: their feet were firm on the ground, they were driven by a deadly logic.

There were the people to consider, the *ra'ayat*, the proles. Their lot would not be improved. The *kampong*-life, the *padi*-planting, the fishing, the magic, the superstitious mumbling of the Koran, the poverty—these would continue. And the rulers would be far from them, forging with pain a new language, apt for governmental directives, which the peasant would not understand. Malay hegemony would mean nothing to the real Malay.

Now, in the twilight of their rule, the Abang began to feel a sort of warmth towards the British. Haughty, white, fat, ugly, by no means *sympathique*, cold, perhaps avaricious—you could call them all these things, but Malaya would be empty without them. The common enemy was also the common law-giver; coldness could mean justice. It was too late to be friendly, too late to try to learn. But one could at least dislike with sympathy and smile through one's valedictory jeers.

Today, he remembered, a white woman was coming to lunch with him. Perhaps she would be the last of the series but, in a sense, the first. Soon he might be living in her world, himself the exile. He would treat her kindly, he would revere her as a symbol, his seduction of her would be civilised, delayed. He would send his best car for her, his politest chauffeur.

The Abang left his apartments and descended the polished staircase—no hazard for bare feet—and sought, at the back of the Istana, the royal garages. There lay his stud of polished darlings, the belamped streamlined docile monsters of years of collecting. Syces were cleaning them down, whistling. Daimler, Buick, Rolls, Bentley, Jaguar, Austin Princess, Hudson—names like a roll of heroines. Every known breed except an Abelard. That was to come. He had already ascertained that the one recently arrived in the State was in excellent condition, with four brand-new tyres. Curiously enough, it was owned by the husband of the white woman coming to lunch. Well, perhaps this would be his last acquisition. It was somewhat unjust that one man had to be wronged twice, but that was probably symbolic: the Prawns or Shrimps or whatever their ridiculous fishy name was, had to be the last sacrifice, because they were the last in. No new expatriates would come to Dahaga now, except perhaps for Indonesian philologists or theologians, and the Lobsters or Crayfish were a sort of tangible twilight.

Drizzle began to mewl out of a dark marine sky. He would play chess with the Sultan. The old boy would appreciate it, poor hag-ridden stooge. The Abang walked to the Sultan's wing. Entering it, he saw in the open office of the A.D.C. the Muslim date. The fasting month was not far off now, and perhaps he had better not covet wives or goods during that time of holy abstinence. The Crabs— it must be Crabs—would have to be cracked open soon. He would send a formal request for the Abelard today, when the Buick went to collect the gold-haired wife.

The Sultan sat alone, wearing a sports-shirt and an old sarong, biting his nails. He grinned up at his visitor.

"What news, *tuanku*? News good?" said the Abang.

"News good."

"Like play chess?"

"Can."

They set out the pieces on the huge board—the elephants, the *hajis*, the horses, the chief minister towering above the impotent raja. While the rain beat at the windows, above the noise of typing, the song from the kitchens, they played, and the Abang played badly. He was not surprised at being beaten—it was all somehow symbolic. The Sultan grinned triumph when he ranged his second elephant next to his first, cutting off retreat from the Abang's raja.

"*Sah-mat!*"

"Yes. Raja dead."

"Not play well today. Why?"

"Not know. Will be time to learn. Much time."

10

"Tell me," said Crabbe, "would you say I was fat?"

The mosquitoes were biting badly tonight—it was an ankle-slapping evening—and there were flying-ant wings in the whisky glasses.

Hardman scrutinised jowl and waistline with careful pale eyes. "Not exactly fat. I should imagine you've put on a bit of weight since you came here. Of course, at the university you were what I'd call an ascetic type—lean jaw and concave belly. Now, well, neither of us is getting any younger. Can you pull that in?"

"Oh, yes. Easily."

"H'm."

Fenella had gone to bed early, fretful, out of sorts. People were always saying this was no climate for a white woman.

"Why this sudden concern about adiposity?" asked Hardman.

"Oh, it was something Fenella said. She said all I thought about was my fat guts, and that I didn't give a damn about her, and that I was becoming hoggish and boorish and thick-skinned. You know the sort of thing—you're a married man."

"I don't get that from Normah. At least, I don't think so. She speaks a bit too fast for me at times."

"More whisky?"

"Thanks."

In the *kampong* the drums were beating for a wedding or a funeral. In the kitchen Ah Wing washed up his many platters, singing an endless plainchant. The cicadas triple-tongued—tickity-tickity—and a big beetle clumsily boomed and beat the wall.

"You're sure you don't mind my asking Georges to come here?"

"Delighted. I'm afraid my French isn't what it used to be, though."

"That hasn't got fat."

"No." Crabbe drank, brooded a moment, and said, "We had a bit of trouble. Apparently she made some damned silly arrangement about having lunch at the Istana. I wouldn't let her go. I think I did the right thing."

"Oh, yes, you did the right thing."

"But then she started saying she never had any fun, that she was stuck out here with nothing to do, surrounded by a lot of half-washed peasants."

"They're a very clean people."

"That's what I said. Anyway, she accused me of carrying on with women, and that she was expected to be the good little stay-at-home, having no fun."

"Why the plural?"

"What plural? Oh, that. It's something that happened in Kuala Hantu. I've been a model of fidelity since."

"Yes." Hardman grinned. "So I've noticed."

"Look here, I'm a bit worried about this Abang. He sent a car round for her at lunch-time, and I had a hell of a job getting rid of it. I said that *mem* couldn't go, she had fever. Strangely enough, she's developed a touch of it this evening."

"All these sandflies. And you've certainly got a good

line in mosquitoes up here." He smacked his neck. "That's another one less."

"But I couldn't get that driver to go away. He'd have stayed all afternoon if I hadn't given him five dollars. And he gave me this."

Hardman opened the large crested envelope and translated slowly to himself:

From the Abang, Scourge of the Wicked, Medicine of the Sick, Comforter of the Afflicted, Money of the Poor, Hope of the Impotent, etc., etc., Greetings.

It has graciously pleased the Abang to be desirous of adding your motor-car to his collection, the which is known to be a wonder and a prodigy in the whole of the Eastern world. A fair price will be given. Be so good as to deliver the vehicle at your earliest convenience, together with all relevant documents, so that transference of ownership may be officially effected in due pursuance of the regulations.

From the Istana, Kenching, the 12th day of the month Shaaban, in the year of the Hijrah, 1374.

"What do they want of us?" said Crabbe. "They work us to death, and they also want our wives and our chattels. It's a bit thick, to say the least. What's the legal position?"

"As far as your wife's having lunch with him is concerned? That, of course, is entirely up to you, or her. She knows what will happen, of course?"

"I've told her. But all women say that they can take care of themselves. She says he's got nice eyes and he wouldn't do anything he shouldn't."

"Yes. As far as the car's concerned, that's entirely up to you again. He's merely inviting you to sell him your car."

"He's not. He's ordering me to sell it. And there's no reference to an actual price."

"It says 'a fair price'. That means presumably what any reputable garage would give you for it. Of course, you'd have to wait for your money."

"How long?"

"Indefinitely."

"And if I refuse to sell?"

"They find some excuse for throwing you out of the State."

"I see." They both drank whisky. Insect activity went merrily, indifferently, on over the crass bourdon of the drums. Ah Wing filed the last of his plates and went singing away to the mysteries of his own quarters. A Malay elder crawled on to the veranda, greeted Crabbe with an edentulous "*Tabek!*" and then crouched in a dark corner, chewing a quid of sireh with hard gums.

"It's a hard life," said Crabbe, "to say the least of it."

"Oh, it is."

"Is there nothing I can do?"

"Don't let him get your wife alone. He'll exercise his *droit de seigneur* with as much ceremony as an orang-outang."

"That means keeping her in purdah."

"In a sense, that's true. If she joined Islam she'd be safe, of course. The Abang is deeply religious."

"Then *I'd* have to become a Muslim, too?"

"Quite right. You'd be in a better position all round if you did. You'd be in the family."

"And how do you like being in the family?"

"As far as the car is concerned, I'd just temporise. Reply

114

courteously to this letter, tell him you're only too delighted to sell him the car, but there are one or two things that have to be put right first, because you wouldn't like him to receive it in a condition unbefitting his exalted position and his known connoisseurship. That kind of thing."

"And how long can I do that for?"

"Till your transfer comes through."

"But I can't apply for a transfer after being here only a couple of months."

"Who said anything about applying?"

"Have you been hearing something?"

The squeal of the wheels of a trishaw outside, and then Father Laforgue was mounting the steps of the veranda. He apologised volubly for being late. The creaking engine of Crabbe's French was cranked up slowly while Hardman gurgled away with a wealth of easy idiom.

"Whisky, *mon père?*"

"Tank you."

"How is the work, Georges?"

"Not bad. I have finished Wang Ch'ung. It is interesting to compare with Han Fei. There is much research to do there."

"And the parish?"

"It goes. You, I believe, *monsieur,* have an old parishioner of mine in your school. Mahalingam is his name. I lost him when he married a Malay girl. He was an indifferent Catholic. He is perhaps now an indifferent Muslim."

"*Je ne sais pas. Il est malade.*"

"Oh, yes?" Father Laforgue showed little interest: Mahalingam was no longer one of his patients.

Conversation did not go well. Father Laforgue tried to speak English and Crabbe tried to speak French. He brought up the topic of birth control and the need to enforce it in the pullulating East.

"*Saya ingat,* I mean, *je pense qu'il faut l'introduire* . . ."

"Church say it not O.K. God say it not O.K." But he was not very interested. Nor did Hardman and he have much to say to each other. It was as though religion had shut a door between them. Crabbe called for more ice. When Ah Wing toddled in, bow-legged, a mummy, all wrinkles and tendons, Father Laforgue greeted him with enthusiasm in words that sounded to Crabbe like vibraphone strokes. Ah Wing replied in an old man's happy lunatic sing-song. Father Laforgue was delighted.

"It is very, very close, his dialect, to that of my old province." He pinged away and Ah Wing, shading his deaf ear with a hollowed hand, listened avidly, half-comprehending, and pinged back. "Is it in order," asked Father Laforgue, "if I ask him to sit down?"

"Well . . ."

"It might give him ideas above his station," said Hardman.

"I understand. The English are very particular on these matters. Perhaps we could go away to his kitchen for a short while and talk there?" Father Laforgue, arm round Ah Wing's shoulders, went off happily, leaving his full glass of whisky and water to the flying ants.

"What have you heard?" resumed Crabbe.

"Oh, I haven't heard anything. But I've just got a feeling you won't last long out here."

"Why not?"

"Enemies. You have enemies."

"Oh, that." Crabbe sat back in relief. "I thought you meant real enemies. I mean, Jaganathan's nothing. . . ."

"All your enemies are real enough," said Hardman.

"They're out to get you, every one of you. The white man's day is coming to an end. *Götterdämmerung*. You've had it."

"You talk as though you're no longer a white man." Crabbe looked at the bloodless face, pale hair, rabbit's eyes.

"I'm not. I have a stake in the country. I can never be thrown out. I shall retire some day, having made my pile out of honest practice, and perhaps go and live in the south of France. Till then, and it may not be all that far off, I shall be respected as a Malayan, a good son of Islam, a hard worker who keeps his money in the country. You know what they call you expatriates? White leeches."

"And are you making much money?"

Hardman moved his thin shoulders. "Not yet. I haven't had much of a chance yet. There's a bit of competition, you know. There's this new Chinese lawyer with the Balliol accent. But I shall win through. It's something to look as though you're making money. I've got a Jaguar. I've got some decent clothes. I don't have to worry too much about dunning people for fees. All that inspires confidence." He poured himself more whisky, his mended mouth set complacently. Crabbe felt a slight stir of distaste.

"Has it been worth it?"

"Has what been worth it?"

"Your marrying a Malay widow, your giving up the European way of life, your complete deracination."

"I'm digging in here. I shall have roots."

"But think of European architecture, and the art galleries, and London on a wet day, river fog, the country in autumn, pubs decorated for Christmas, book-shops, a live symphony orchestra . . ."

"The exile's dream of home," grinned Hardman. "My dear Victor, what a sea-change. Is this our old ruthless dialectician, our hard-as-nails pillar of pure reason? You *must* be getting fat, you know."

'God,' thought Crabbe, 'I'm talking like Fenella. What devil made me do that?'

"There speaks the old Empire-builder," said Hardman. "You're a bit late, old man. You've only got to the third drama of the cycle. After the grubbing for Rhinegold come the thundering hoofs. And then Rhodes and Raffles, Siegfrieds in armour and bad verse. And always this ghastly 'What do they know of England?' Why did you come out here?"

"I told you before," said Crabbe wearily.

"I know. You spouted some nonsense about heliotropism and applying for a job when you were tight. How about the metaphysical level, the level of ideas? I mean, knowing you, unless you've changed all that much. . . ."

"Well," Crabbe puffed at a cigarette that was damp with the night air, "I suppose part of me thought that England was all television and strikes and nobody giving a damn about culture. I thought they needed me more out here."

"They didn't need you. They needed somebody else, and only long enough to teach them how to manage a strike and erect a television transmitter. And that's not your line, Victor."

"I can teach them how to think. I can inculcate some idea of values."

"You'll never teach them how to think. And you know damn well they've got their own values, and they're not going to change those for any high-minded, pink-kneed colonial officer. They're ready to take over now. It's probably going to be a hell of a mess, but that's not the point. Whether the fruit's going to be good or rotten, the time is ripe."

It was Crabbe's turn to sneer. "And of course there's always the army of unalterable law."

"Not such an army. That's why I'm in a good position. But you can't deny that law is part of the machine. They can do without you, but not without me."

"What do you want me to do then? Go home?"

"Oh, they'll find something for you, for a time, anyway. But not in the history seminar with bright-eyed brown-skins eagerly lapping the milk of culture. You'll become part of the executive engine, easily replaceable when the time comes, and translate nationalist politics into directives for the new leaders of youth. And I shall find that my work is not so ignoble after all. Certainly it'll be rather more creative than yours."

"You've changed, Rupert. Changed a hell of a lot."

"Yes, I've changed. I had a crash at the end of the war, remember, and before that a few years of always expecting to crash. God gave me one face and the war gave me another." He had had four large whiskies and it was beginning to show. "That's why I'm all for Justice. For Law, anyway." He took more whisky. Father Laforgue walked cheerfully back into the silence, a silence loud enough with the busy factory jungle-noise, the hunting cries of the house-lizards, the crack of the beetles against the wall, and still the *kampong* drum.

"He has some remarkable things," he said. "Some remarkable medicines." He held up an aspirin-bottle of vomit-coloured liquid. "He gave me this for the tooth-ache." He sat down and picked up his warm whisky, its surface autumn-littered with ant-wings, and looked at his host and friend contentedly. "He is a very remarkable old man. He lives completely in the past. And he is very kind, he has many of the old Chinese virtues. The Chinese will never let their friends down, and they always help those in need. They always help poor relatives, for instance."

"Doucement," said Crabbe, *"s'il vous plaît.* He speaks too fast for me," he said, turning to Hardman.

"Your servant here," said Father Laforgue, at the same speed but rather more loudly, "sends money regularly to his sister in China, and he is very good even to his son-in-law, who lives in the jungle."

"I still don't quite get that," said Crabbe.

"He helps his son-in-law," said Hardman. "In the jungle."

"His son-in-law is a soldier," said Father Laforgue. "He has a gun and he spends his time shooting in the jungle. But he gets very little food, and your servant sends it to him. That is very strange, of course, because I always understood that soldiers had good rations."

Crabbe began to feel slightly sick.

"He says the aborigines are very helpful because they take the food into the jungle and they give it to your servant's son-in-law and he shares it with his comrades. The Chinese are very generous. Even though I was in one of their prisons for a long time, I can still say that. They are the most generous people in the world. And loyal too." He beamed, not noticing, perhaps because of the shadows, perhaps because of his absorption in the Chinese dream-world, Crabbe's increasing pallor. "I could you tell many stories of how the Chinese have been generous to me. There was, for example, the time when the great wind blew down my small church . . ."

"Now," said Hardman to Crabbe, "you really do need legal advice."

I I

Victor Crabbe went to bed very late, very weary. He, Hardman and Father Laforgue had spent a stuffy hour in Ah
Wing's quarters, where the guileless old man had been
harangued and cross-examined, all to little purpose. The
session had been a linguistic nightmare—English to French
to Chinese or just French to Chinese and then all the way
back again, with reproaches and threats in Malay from
Crabbe, the cries of a wounded bird. Neither priest nor
servant could be convinced that one of the most ghastly
offences against the Emergency Regulations had been committed. Crabbe's head reeled. As in a cotton-wool-padded
world of 'flu delirium, they threw the ball of question and
answer from hand to hand, watching it change shape and
colour, dropping it, losing it, all against a foetid background
of preserved lizards, tiger's teeth and whiskers, ancient
eggs, fat cats, a picture of Sun Yat Sen. At the end of it all
Ah Wing remained unshaken. He sat tailor-wise on his
bed, picking the horny soles of his feet, a fixed smile on his
mouth empty of teeth, now and again nodding delightedly,
often misunderstanding, mishearing. The ball was lost
frequently in the hazards of his deafness. His logic was
simple: if his daughter's husband needed the odd handful
of rice was it not his plain family duty to provide it?
Solidarity. The concept of the State had never even had a
chance to wither away in his mind; the holy Family stood

solid. But, said Crabbe, the Communists were evil, cruel, they wanted to overthrow established order and rule with the rubber truncheon and the firing squad. He even began to tell stories about eviscerations and decapitations. It made no difference. Ah Wing seemed rather pleased than otherwise at the prospect of Red Chinese ruling Malaya. Blood was thicker than ideology. The son-in-law, moreover, was a young man who had always worked hard and had fought bravely against the Japanese. He was a good boy. He the Enemy of Mankind? Nonsense.

It was genuine innocence, the most dangerous thing in the world. Crabbe shook when he considered his own position. He always paid the food bills himself—Fenella was no housekeeper—and he had never troubled to check the invoices. Fenella had, admittedly, once commented on the amount of waste that went on, but Crabbe had taken no notice. Now he had visions of terrorists sitting down to the kippers he sent back uneaten, large joints ravaged by only a few cuttings, cold fried eggs in newspaper, mounds of cooked rice taken back to the kitchen on curry evenings. Ah Wing had not even stolen anything: he had used only the servant's privilege of appropriating rinds, crumbs and tail-ends.

None of the orthodox measures seemed to fit the situation. Ah Wing should be handed over to the police, but then so should Crabbe himself. The Security Forces should be tipped off, and then Crabbe would have some awkward explaining to do. Ah Wing should at least be dismissed, but in his senile innocence he would sooner or later let out his story to a Chinese ear, and there were people, not necessarily Chinese, who would be pleased to see Crabbe convicted of consorting with the enemy. It was not wise to send Ah Wing away from this isolated Eden. He never went to town, he met only Malays with no strong interest in the Emergency, odd Sakais with blow-pipes and the drivers of tradesman's vans. How about the tradesmen themselves? It was unlikely that they would be suspicious, especially as more than one general dealer was patronised by the Crabbes. And even if, in some *kedai* off-duty, shop-keepers spoke of the mountains of meat consumed by the new headmaster, they might well remember the days of lavish dinner-parties and glory that the past had returned. And there was Talbot's great diseased appetite to corroborate a belief that expatriate educationists ate hoggishly. The future could be made safe for Ah Wing's master—reduce the orders at once—but Ah Wing would have to paddle his own sampan. It was the past that worried Crabbe—'EXPAT TEACHER SENT SUPPLIES TO C.T. HIDEOUT'. Presumably Hardman and Father Laforgue could be trusted. But the whole business had been most unfortunate. Only one issue was good: food-bills would be smaller, and Crabbe would lose weight and save money.

Still, he woke to the last of the giant breakfasts with the sour taste of foreboding in his mouth. The morning's work and its many cigarettes helped to confuse the source of the sourness. The term was coming to an end with the approach of the Muslim fasting month, and examination marks were being handed in. One master called (Crabbe could never get over this) Mr. Gunga Din came hotly to state that he had it on unimpeachable evidence that Abdul Kadir had sold examination questions to his class—two dollars a question—and that Crabbe would find this confirmed in the astronomical marks of Abdul Kadir's wealthier pupils. Also Crabbe had read some history answers which glorified a mythical Indian rule in nineteenth-century Malaya and vilified the depraved British who crushed it out:

"Sir Raffles kill many Malays for not paying cruel taxes and build big prison for Malays and Indians and Chinese to be tortured and children have heads cut off by soldiers as cruel joke to laughing English."

Five minutes after the final bell of the morning he was at his desk with a full ash-tray and a sheaf of unintelligible estimates. Mr. Jaganathan, polished and grave, walked in.

"I wish to speak with you, Mr. Crabbe. I think it better we go out to talk, for these Malay clerks know much English. What I have to say is very serious."

"You mean about Abdul Kadir?"

"I think it better we go out to talk."

They went on to the dry grass of the playing-field. The sun rode high and the air was loud with children and home-going bicycle-bells. Mr. Jaganathan, his head dewed by the sun, his armpits spilling over their damp patches, spoke.

"Mr. Crabbe, I have found out all about you."

"I beg your pardon?"

"It is too late to beg pardon, Mr. Crabbe. What I have found out is very, very serious. It is so serious that I will tell nobody. But you will realise there is only one thing you can do."

Crabbe thought: 'It hasn't taken long.' Bitterly he remembered that there can be no secrets in a colonial community. But still he presented to Jaganathan the face of bewilderment, with anger ready to show at any moment.

"Perhaps you had better make yourself clear, Mr. Jaganathan."

"I will make myself clear. Not to mince matters, I will say here and now without preliminaries of any kind whatsoever that I know about your politics."

"A government officer has no politics, Mr. Jaganathan. You have been in the service long enough to know that."

"That makes it all the more worse, Mr. Crabbe, that your politics should be of the kind they are. Not to beat about the bush, Mr. Crabbe, I will say that I have found out you are prominent Communist and that you are here to help Communist terrorists in the jungle under the disguise of teaching the little ones of Malaya."

"That, Mr. Jaganathan, is a most serious accusation. I hope you realise the gravity of what you are saying."

"I realise it all too well, Mr. Crabbe. I realise also the gravity of your being in this school, in charge of innocent minds which it is your intention to corrupt with vile Communist indoctrination."

"I refuse to get angry, Mr. Jaganathan. If what you're saying were not so slanderous I should be tempted to laugh. What evidence have you got to support these wild statements?"

"It is evidence of what was told me by a man who knows you well, Mr. Crabbe. It is a man you have known many years. He studied with you at the same university, and he says even there you were prominent Communist."

"You mean Mr. Hardman?"

"None other, Mr. Crabbe. It is but a matter of very short time indeed that I have it from his word of mouth. Moreover, there was witness in the shape of the gentleman in charge of the aborigines. I am very grieved about all this, Mr. Crabbe." Grief sweated from him all over; his shirt wept with grief.

"I see. And naturally you believe this gentleman?"

"I do not wish to, Mr. Crabbe. But I must think of these poor innocent children."

"Right, Mr. Jaganathan." Crabbe felt more empty than angry. Betrayal has always to be expected. What in God's name had Hardman got against him? Crabbe thought he knew: the old envy of the odd little albino freshman, shy of women, for the successful and prominent third-year student who was engaged to a pretty and talented girl. Envy, too, because Hardman had suffered from the war more than Crabbe had. And then the intrusion on Hardman's new rootless world, on his penury, his eccentric marriage. Hardman had acted quickly. But was all this enough to justify such a betrayal? Perhaps so; one never ceased to learn, never ceased to be astonished.

"Mr. Jaganathan," said Crabbe slowly. "You may do precisely what you please. I do not propose to deny or confirm this allegation to you. If you wish to believe this incredible story, you may. You may act on it as soon as you wish. But remember that you will require evidence, very conclusive evidence. This is a most grave accusation, remember. I would ask you, for your own sake, to think most carefully before you act."

"But, Mr. Crabbe, I do not wish to act. I know it is my duty to do so, but I have read my Shakespeare and I know of the quality of mercy." Mercy rilled down his face, strained through his shirt. "It is quite easy, the thing you have to do. You have merely to ask for a transfer. I do not wish to ruin your career. I only wish you not to be corrupting these poor children here in this school where I have worked so long."

"But, you know, Mr. Jaganathan, you should wish to ruin my career. If I had conclusive evidence that you were a Communist I should immediately start ruining your career. I should go immediately to the police about you. I should only be happy if you were under lock and key."

Mr. Jaganathan smiled in sweaty benignity. "You are a young man, Mr. Crabbe. Perhaps already you learn the error of your ways. Perhaps you do not know precisely what you do. I give you a chance."

"What is your evidence?" asked Crabbe. "Frankly, I believe all this is bluff, Mr. Jaganathan. Ever since I came to the school you've wanted me out of it. This is your first full-dress attempt to drive me away. You can't do it, you know. You know as well as I, that there's nothing in this damned silly piece of slander. Hardman's got something against me, so have you. You say I'm a Communist. All right, I could say the same about you, about the Abang, the Sultan, the High Commissioner. But I've got to have evidence, strong evidence. You know damn well that you wouldn't dare go to the police about this business. It's just sheer unscrupulous nastiness, and you're going to suffer for this. . . ." His temper was rising too fast. He gulped, stopped. Jaganathan calmed him with a smile and gesture.

"There, there, Mr. Crabbe. It is not good that you lose your control like that. This is very bad climate for losing control. I see your heart beating through your shirt. Now just go home and lie down for a little while and rest and think of what I have said. I can be your friend, Mr. Crabbe. I ask very, very little, and then you are perfectly safe with me. Now go and rest, Mr. Crabbe, rest, rest, rest." Crabbe felt listless, hearing the sing-song soothing voice, remembering another time when Jaganathan had counselled rest, in that same voice, remembering Talbot's words about the 'magic boys'. He raised his eyes to Jaganathan's, but found he was squinting into the sun, that he could not look at Jaganathan. It was all bloody nonsense, of course.

"You'll suffer for this, Jaganathan," he said. "By God, you will."

"You will suffer, Mr. Crabbe, if you are not more sensible. You go home now and rest, and then write a short note to Kuala Lumpur asking for a transfer. It is quite simple. You have never liked it here, Mr. Crabbe, you have always hated it. You will be happier somewhere else, much, much happier."

Crabbe stumbled off, up the grass slope, to his car, trying to think. Evidence. Suppose Hardman maliciously got hold of Ah Wing and used the innocent Father Laforgue to interpret, suppose he gave Jaganathan that first-hand evidence. . . . Suppose, worse, he contacted the Security Forces and got them to watch for the next Sakai emissaries, to seek out the path to the hide-out. Why, why, why? Did Hardman want him out of the way so badly? Did he want to wreck his career? What was the real motive behind it? Or was it just some peculiar malice, age-old, living in this primitive State, demons older than Islam or even Hinduism, exiled to the jungle, working silently through the axe-men, the magicians, the betrayers of friends, the men who were, almost despite themselves, cruel to their wives, as he was to Fenella?

He arrived home to find the table set for one, and on the table a folded note.

"The Abang called personally and asked me to go with him to the Bedebah Waterfalls. I didn't see why not. I may be late. Don't worry. F."

Crabbe ate his way grimly through the last of the huge Edwardian luncheons—ox-tail soup, grilled sole, Scotch eggs, beef and four vegetables, caramel cream, Camembert. He eyed with something near to hate the happily chirping Ah Wing. He tried warning him again, but his Malay was not of a kind that Ah Wing understood, and he knew no Chinese. Ah Wing nodded brightly, crowing assent to he knew not what, going off singing to the kitchen. After lunch Crabbe sat around, restless, trying to read, sour-faced even at the rhythmic haunches of Fatimah, the young amah, who undulated down to the bedroom with an armful of laundered clothes. Empty time stretched before him— afternoon school was a loud chant of Koran and vernacular languages, outside the white man's province—and he needed Fenella now, perhaps, he realised, for the first time for a long time.

He was lonely, worried. He ought to contact Hardman and have it out with him, but that was no work for an afternoon fainting with heat. Perhaps he ought to drive down to the Waterfalls and confront the Abang. Finally he decided to go and see Anne Talbot. Talbot would certainly be in his office and Anne would certainly be at home. He wanted comfort, even the comfort of that apneumatic bosom and those thin thighs.

He found she was ready enough to give comfort. They wore the afternoon away, sweating in the fanless bed-room, at last drowsing while a cock crowed near-by and the sea beat and the coconut palms rustled with quest-ing *beroks*. Meanwhile, in the sun-hot town, three Sikhs drank.

"Brother," said Kartar Singh, "that your business does not prosper is a sign. It is a sign that trade is an ignoble occupation for men of our race. It is God himself telling you that buying and selling ill befit a warrior son of the great Guru. Brother, get out while there is time. Our life is service, not gain. We, the warriors, protect the weaker and more timid citizenry of the shops and offices, by night as well as by day." Gracefully he had acknowledged the value of Teja Singh's supine occupation. Teja Singh, mindful of the courtesy, raised his glass of *samsu* and solemnly drank.

"It is competition," said Mohinder Singh. "The Chinese and Bengalis and Tamils are men of no honour. They sell too cheap. But, misguided, the fools of the town patronise them. I am losing money, brothers, I am losing it fast."

"What is money?" said Kartar Singh. "It is nothing."

"It is useful for buying *samsu*," said Teja Singh.

"Come," said Kartar Singh, "we will have a song." He raised his tuneless voice in a doubtful ballad:

> "Beasts and men are made the same—
>   Here a one and there a two,
>   And with these three they play the game
>   Of doing what they have to do."

Two Malay workmen, dish-towels round their heads, came in to drink iced water.

"There they go, hairy sods, drinking all day."

"Doing no work."

"Let them have their pleasure. They won't have it much longer."

"The reckoning is coming."

"Shit for brains."

"Like prawns."

The *samsu* flowed freely. Kartar Singh had overlooked a parking offence that day, and the grateful Chinese driver had slipped him five dollars. As the magical flower of the brief twilight lulled them, the yodel of the muezzin turning to Mecca, the lights coming on in the shops, only Mohinder Singh felt morose.

"I have failed," he said. "Failed. Here am I grateful for the hospitality of a police constable, when it is I who should be crowding this table with bottles."

"And so you will, brother, so you will. It is not too late to start again. In the police there are many opportunities. And," he nodded his great beard at Teja Singh, "also even in the night watchman's profession."

"It is now we need money," said Teja Singh. "I have but thirty cents. The bottle is empty."

The scanty ration of intellect that sweltered in Kartar Singh's monumental fat today had determined to expend itself. What the hell.

"The white woman, brother," he cried. "Have you forgotten? Have you forgotten that she wants to buy up your shop? Camphorwood chests and blankets and sheets and cutlery and plates. We will go to her house. We will take these things to her. We shall be paid. We may even be offered whisky."

"Can we?" Mohinder Singh was sapped of confidence. "We may be turned away. And then we shall have wasted trishaw fares and also have lost face."

"Lose face? It is only the cowardly Chinese who talk of that. We Sikhs are men of courage, of adventure. If we fail, we fail. But we shall not fail."

Kartar Singh was exhibiting signs of a talent for salesmanship. He was showing enterprise. Mohinder Singh did not like this.

"I think it is not a good idea," he said.

"And so you will drink all day at my expense, and when the chance is given you to repay hospitality you will not take it. That I call the attitude of an ingrate."

"It was you who persuaded me to come and drink. I was unwilling."

"'Not so unwilling. You needed only three minutes' persuading."

"You will remember that before you lost me valuable trade. It was inconsiderate, to say the least."

"It was *this* trade, brother, trade that you seem anxious to lose without any help from me or anyone else."

"Are you implying . . ."

"Brothers, brothers," soothed Teja Singh, "we must not quarrel."

"No, we will not quarrel," said Kartar Singh. "I accept his apology. Come, we will go. We will have a little adventure."

They staggered down to the shop, unlocked it with difficulty, and then called loudly for trishaws. Soon they were loading goods on to them, while the mummified Chinese druggist next door looked on sardonically.

"I knew you would never make a shopkeeper. You take too much time off."

"These," said Kartar Singh, "we are selling. We will beat you towkays at your own game. We seek custom in the highways and by-ways. We do not sit on our bottoms, picking our teeth, waiting for people to come. We go to them." Kartar Singh, this one night, was inspired.

"So he is not closing down?"

"We are not closing down," said Kartar Singh. After all his talk about the ignominy of trade, Mohinder Singh did not like this new proprietorial attitude, this lordly plurality. But he said nothing. Clumsily they loaded three trishaws with miscellaneous goods. They locked the shop. They called for two further trishaws—one for Teja Singh and Mohinder Singh, one for Kartar Singh. Again Mohinder Singh did not like this, though it was evident that the policeman's great bulk could not be accommodated in less than a full seat. Still, Mohinder Singh would have much preferred it if he himself had led the procession in lone comfort, instead of being pressed against the crumpled and grubby person of one who was, after all, and all questions of racial solidarity aside, his social inferior. It was certainly not pleasant either to see Kartar Singh taking charge of the sweating and swaying cortège like some gross god of wine re-arisen, bringing fatness and loud words to the humble village folk.

At one point on the dark road the camphorwood chest crashed to the dust, but helpful *kampong* boys restored it to its seat. Later a roll of muslin fell and unwound snakily. But to Kartar Singh's simple heroic soul these mishaps were part of some picaresque adventure, a pretext for plump laughter and even song.

At length they reached the house of the Crabbes, a civilised outpost among crude Malay dwellings. "See," said Kartar Singh in triumph, "the lights are lit. They will now be drinking their whisky before the evening meal. We will provide diversion. We will be welcome and offered refreshment. Was I not right, brothers, to suggest this small excursion? Will it not bring us both pleasure and profit?"

But, mounting to the veranda, they were amazed to see great activity and to hear loud Chinese words and Malay screams. "Surely," said Teja Singh, "that Chinese is not lord of the house. Certainly it is not seemly for him to be chasing a young girl like that."

"Ha," said Kartar Singh, "that young girl I know. She is the daughter of Abu Bakar. He was in the police with me, a corporal. I have seen her often at his house. Now what is that old man trying to do?"

"She is carrying a black cat," said Mohinder Singh.

"That will afford her little protection."

The pursuer and pursued disappeared down a dark corridor. The pursued reappeared from another direction, screaming and still clutching the black cat. Ah Wing, not yet winded, was soon after her.

"Here we must step in," said Kartar Singh bravely. "What he is doing is not right." From his left breast pocket he produced a whistle and blew it. Then he strode into the house, followed by his friends. In a solid heavy-bearded line they confronted Ah Wing. The girl fled to her quarters.

"Are you not ashamed?" said Kartar Singh. "An old man like you, and a girl so young and defenceless."

He spoke in Malay. Ah Wing replied in the same tongue, or an obscure version of it, and the only intelligible word was '*Makan*'.

'*Makan*' has too many meanings. It primarily means to eat, but it is often used of the action of the cock and the hen, the bull and the cow, supererogatory in a language rich in motor and sensory terms. Kartar Singh, his one rare day of imagination not yet set, took this secondary meaning. He forgot that the Malays revere cats and that the Chinese merely relish them. He wagged a solemn finger at Ah Wing, warning him, telling him that the sins of the flesh were the last to be forgiven. Then, seeming to relent, he said, "We have come to see your master. We will wait. Bring us refreshment."

Ah Wing seemed not to understand, so Teja Singh used two words of the universal language, potent words on which the sun never sets.

"Police. Whisky."

Ah Wing scuttled off. The Sikhs sat in lordly ease on the veranda. *Kampong* dwellers appeared, curious, responding tardily to the whistle. Kartar Singh addressed them.

"It is nothing. The police have everything under control. It is but this foolish old Chinese seeking to cover a virgin and thus regain lost youth. That is their superstition. Ah, my old friend Abu Bakar. It is a long time since we last met. Yes, your daughter. Ha ha, it is nothing. This old Chinese was after her. But we got here in time. The Sikhs are always in time."

His words had some effect. Murmuring began. Tough swarthy faces turned to each other in glottal complaint. But two days before there had been a small Sino–Malay brush-up in the town: two Malay workmen, turban dish-cloths on their heads, had seen a Chinese at his evening meal and accused him of eating pork. A row had started; other Malays had appeared; the eater—who had been con-suming innocent *halal* market beef—called on his sons to come from the back of the shop and support him. Hard words had been exchanged; the police came. In the minds of some who heard of the incident there grew the notion that the day of wrath was at hand; the hour when the Malays should be freed of their Chinese creditors was approaching; independence would soon be here. The guileless Ah Wing was now in an awkward position, especially as the suitor of the young amah, Fatimah, heard the words of Kartar Singh. He was a young carpenter and, in his spare time, a shadow-play master. Often he had prayed to the ox-hide figure of Pa' Dogok, hero of the ancient Hindu legends which he nightly presented, to soften the heart of the haughty maiden. And now a Chinese, an old one at that, a pork-stuffing pincered crab, had dared to attempt what he himself blushed to dream of. Anger rose in the crowd. There was talk of axes.

"I beg you," said Kartar Singh, "not to take this further. He did nothing. I came in time. I have punished him with

my tongue. That was sharper than any axe. I beg you . . .
Law and order . . . I shall be forced to blow my whistle
again. . . ."

"*Besok,*" called somebody. "Tomorrow." The cry was
taken up.

"Tonight," called another. "*Malam ini.*"

"Not tonight," said Kartar Singh. "I shall blow my
whistle."

The crowd dispersed murmuring. But Ah Wing, listening in his quarters, heard certain dread key-words. He had
known that the Malays did not approve of eating cats, but
surely axeing was going a little too far?

"He is a long time coming with that whisky," said Teja
Singh.

"And where are the white people?" asked Mohinder
Singh. "It is already late and they have not come for their
meal. For my part, I could eat something."

"What is his name?" said Teja Singh. "Call him."

"Did I not do well?" said Kartar Singh. "Do you not
think I quelled the mob efficiently?"

"We had better go," said Mohinder Singh. "They are
not coming. We have waited long enough. I told you this
was not a good idea."

"There is always tomorrow," said Kartar Singh. "We
will come again tomorrow. Still, we did not come in vain.
I did my duty."

The trishaw drivers rang impatient bells. The three
Sikhs descended.

"Gone," cried Mohinder Singh. "The camphorwood
chest. It is gone."

"And the roll of cloth," said Teja Singh. "That is gone,
too."

"Boy," cried Mohinder Singh to one of the drivers, "what

136

do you know of this? Who has been thieving here?"

All the drivers looked blank.

"This is all your fault again," raged Mohinder Singh to the fat constable. "It is always your fault. Every time you force me to come out with you something goes wrong. Now perhaps you are content. I am ruined."

"You will not use that language to me," said Kartar Singh. "You will not accuse me in that manner."

"You have ruined me. I always knew you would. That has been your intention."

"You will not speak like that. . . ."

"You fat pig. You bladder of disgusting lard . . ."

"If you dare . . ."

"The boys want their money," said Teja Singh. "They will not take us back until they have been paid."

"Friend! Heaven preserve me from such friends. . . ."

"I will use violence. . . ."

"You would not know how to. . . ."

"Have a care. . . ."

Teja Singh quietly gave to one of the trishaw drivers the remains of a tea-set. In lieu of cash. Quietly he drove off in the dark to his work. He left the other two to their argument. His night-watchman's bed awaited him. The day had tired him out; he stretched in delicious anticipation of a night's honest toil.

12

She had absolutely no right to go off like that, especially after all the trouble he had had the previous day, telling lies and dispensing dollars. Didn't she realise that she was making an absolute fool of him, the laughing-stock of the town, didn't she know the Abang's reputation, didn't she realise that he had only one aim in mind, and by God he would fulfil that aim before very long if Crabbe did not prevent him?

Or had he fulfilled it already?

How dare he indulge in such nasty insinuations! The Abang had been charming, attentive, a model of propriety. Whatever his reputation was, it was something of a change to receive such attentions after all these months, nay years, in which she might as well have been a dirty clothes basket for all the notice her husband took of her. Plenty of time to chase other women, no time at all for his own wife. And for all his promises, it was still going on.

What was still going on?

Oh, she wasn't such a fool. She saw what was happening under her very nose. Making eyes at Anne Talbot, she recognised all the symptoms. If he was going to live his own life she was going to live hers. Did he not realise that he had not evinced the slightest desire to make love to his own wife for months now? She had been losing confidence in herself; now at last a little of it was being regained. If he didn't think she was attractive there were others who did. And so on.

Friday and a school holiday. But Crabbe was awake and up early, long before the time of the bedside tray, aware that something had changed, that something was wrong. In shorts, sandals and a Hawaiian shirt, unwashed and unshaven, he went to the kitchen and found it cool and deserted. He called Ah Wing but there was no reply. Perhaps he was ill, perhaps—he swiftly quelled the cruel hope —the old man had died in his sleep. He knocked at Ah Wing's door, once, twice, then tried the handle. It was unlocked. The room was empty of all the old eggs and lizards and horrible medicines that furnished Ah Wing's life. Only a picture of Sun Yat Sen remained on the wall, staring glassy-eyed at the new China, amid the smells of the old. Ah Wing had vanished.

Crabbe called Fatimah. Soon she appeared, hair down her back, plump young brown shoulders naked above the sarong she was knotting under her arms. After her sidled a black cat, mewing.

"*Tuan?*"

"Where is Ah Wing?"

"Gone, *tuan*. Taken all his belongings."

Where had he gone? She did not know. All she knew was that two aborigines in torn shirts and nothing else had come to the back of the house late the previous night and Ah Wing had followed them. She had not wanted to disturb *Tuan* and *Mem* in the middle of their quarrel to tell them of this.

"Why did he go?"

"*Dia takut kapak kechil, tuan.*"

So he was frightened of the little axes, was he? Crabbe began to feel an enormous relief welling up in him, like warm blood after a cold shower. Ah Wing had gone, presumably to join his son-in-law in the jungle, to chirp happily over the cooking-pot among snakes and leeches and rusting rifles, gone out of Crabbe's life for ever. Why he feared the axes Crabbe did not trouble to ask: everybody found cause to fear the axes sooner or later. It was providential that Ah Wing had found cause to fear them at this particular moment of time. Crabbe, elated, would have flung his arms around the desirable plump body of Fatimah and kissed the moist bee-stung lips in gratitude for the words of release they had uttered had he not also fear of the axes. He merely smiled and went back to the kitchen to boil the kettle for tea.

As he sat drinking it and eating bread and marmalade he thought: 'Now, Mr. Jaganathan, you can do your damnedest. And, Mr. Hardman, you have it coming to you as well.' There was nothing anyone could do now: the jungle road was closed, the thread of the labyrinth was broken, the tangible evidence had been devoured by the huge green mouth of the forest, and the teeth had snapped shut. And Crabbe himself would celebrate his new-found security with a brief holiday in Kuala Lumpur, in the willing arms of Anne Talbot.

He went back to the bedroom and woke Fenella rudely.

"We've no cook. If you want breakfast you'll have to get it yourself. I'm going off to see Jaganathan."

"No cook? What do you mean?"

"Ah Wing has left. Don't ask me why. He's just gone, that's all."

"You seem very pleased about it."

"I am."

Jaganathan's house was a sweltering wooden structure half-way between the College and the town. When Crabbe drew up before it he heard the loud noise of a Tamil day that had long started. Outside the house black pot-bellied children shrieked and tumbled; from within came the sound of loud female scolding. A large dog—brown, shapeless, old but visibly dentate—stretched its chain to taut metal and cursed Crabbe.

"Good dog, good dog. Come on, shake paws, blast you."

Mr. Jaganathan came to the door, a black flabby sweating chest above a tartan sarong. He greeted Crabbe affably and bade him enter.

"I can't."

"The English are said to be so fond of dogs." Indulgently, Mr. Jaganathan grasped the thick studded collar of the growling hound and let Crabbe go in.

The living-room was full of children, mostly naked. One small boy was eating a cold chapatti on the dusty floor, a baby lying on the dining table, cried piteously for the breast. Jaganathan led Crabbe to an alcove and shooed away two marriageable girls in saris who were seated quietly at their homework. With wide hospitable gestures Jaganathan showed Crabbe to a chair, and the two men looked at each other over a glass-topped table in which were embedded family snapshots, cut-outs of Indian film stars and a Chinese mineral water advertisement.

"You have been thinking, Mr. Crabbe, as I advised you?"

"Oh, yes, Mr. Jaganathan."

"It is very hot day. We do not have fans in this class of government quarters. You would like a refreshing drink, Mr. Crabbe? I have whisky."

"No, thank you, Mr. Jaganathan." They always began their interviews thus, with a great travesty of politeness.

"And what conclusion have you come to, Mr. Crabbe?"

"That I am most certainly not going to do as you suggest,

Mr. Jaganathan. That if one of us is to go, it is certainly not going to be me."

Jaganathan smiled winningly, and said, "I think we will both have some whisky, Mr. Crabbe. I have some bottles of soda outside in the well. They should be cool enough."

"You drink by all means, Mr. Jaganathan. Not for me, thank you."

Jaganathan called loudly and a trembling boy appeared. "This fellow is my eldest son," said Jaganathan. "He is a good-for-nothing. He is only fit to run errands and do work of a menial." Jaganathan spoke loud burring Tamil, hit the boy on the head, and then watched him run off.

"The other day, Mr. Crabbe, you talked of evidence. Today I will show you my evidence."

"Show?"

"Yes, Mr. Crabbe. I have a brother-in-law in Singapore. He is in the library of the University there. The University receives publications of all the big universities in England, Mr. Crabbe. I asked him to do little research, Mr. Crabbe, and he looked up all back numbers of the magazine of your University Union, Mr. Crabbe. The result is most interesting."

A naked female child came round to Crabbe, drooling. Mr. Jaganathan took the child on his knee, watching, with pride, its slow dribble.

"You wrote many articles, Mr. Crabbe, on universal necessity for Communism."

"Did I, Mr. Jaganathan? You know, I'd completely forgotten."

"Now you will remember, Mr. Crabbe."

Crabbe began to feel a certain disappointment. Was this, then, to be the evidence? Jaganathan called loudly again, and again the boy appeared, this time carrying a whisky bottle and a brief-case. Jaganathan roared with anger and cuffed the boy.

"The fool brings neither glasses nor soda-water."

"Unlike some of your Hindu gods, Mr. Jaganathan, he would appear to have only two hands."

"Now, Mr. Crabbe, pardon me one moment." He put the naked child down on the floor. It crawled over to Crabbe and began to dribble on to his sandals. Jaganathan opened the brief-case and extracted a brochure with a red cover. Crabbe's heart turned over as the past came hurtling back. It was a copy of *Vista*, the undergraduate magazine to which he himself had in fact often contributed, had, for one year, edited. How strange that here, eight thousand miles and a whole life away, part of one's past should be recorded, waiting to spring out at one in a Tamil house full of bawling children, hens clucking outside, the fat black sweating hand holding it out. How very strange.

"Look at it, Mr. Crabbe, and decide whether this is not evidence. And not this only. There are other issues in which you have written on this same topic."

"This is a long, long time ago, Mr. Jaganathan."

"It seems not long. It was in that year that I first came to teach at Haji Ali College. Look at it well, Mr. Crabbe."

Crabbe looked at it well. His heart turned over again as he opened it at an article entitled 'Stravinsky and the Tradition'. The name of the writer of the article . . . He breathed heavily, felt faint.

"You see, Mr. Crabbe. You have done very, very foolish thing."

And here a poem by Hardman, a very bad poem. Crabbe saw a blur of print only before he steadied himself to look at it.

The one woman I long for,
Straight as an apple tree,
And in her voice all summer,
Bird and breeze and bee.

And then an article by Victor Crabbe, arrogant, ignorant, juvenile:

> The deterministic principle that Marx took over from Hegel is often lost sight of by those who work for the cause. The class struggle is inevitable, an ineluctable part of the dialectical process, and the revolution, however slow its coming, nevertheless has to come. . . .

"And here, Mr. Crabbe, you talk of the Communist revolution in the East. You say that that is next important arena where standard of living is lowest in the world. You also say . . ."

"It was a long time ago," said Crabbe faintly. He took out his handkerchief and mopped his left eye. "A very long time ago."

"I see you are overcome by shame, Mr. Crabbe. For that reason I do not wish to be too hard. You have only to do as I say."

"How little you understand," said Crabbe. "That's a dead world. That was another me. We all believed in it then. It was our new myth, our new hope. It was all very foolish."

"Very foolish. And now you are beginning to see consequence of your foolishness."

And she too, dark hair, blue jumper, sitting beside him on the floor, drinking tea, occasionally adding her voice to the discussion. Once, to the group, she had played records of Mossolov and Shostakovitch.

144

"Oh, God, man," cried Crabbe, "it was wholesome, it was good, it was youth. It was right for us then. We wanted to improve the world. We honestly thought that we loved mankind. Perhaps we did. Oh, we found out that we'd been following a false god, but at the time it seemed the only religion for a man of any feeling or intelligence. Those articles represent a part of me that I'm not at all ashamed of. I wouldn't retract them. They were true for that stage in my development. But they don't represent me now."

"You say you wouldn't retract them, Mr. Crabbe?"

"Jaganathan, you're a bloody fool. I'd be doing a great disservice to Malay if I got out and let you take over."

"You will kindly not call me bloody fool in my own house, Mr. Crabbe." Jaganathan shook. "Who are you to say I could not run this school? I was running this school when you were still writing your wicked articles about the necessity of Communist bandits in the East. While you were only a foolish young soldier I was running this school."

"Were your masters pleased with you, Mr. Jaganathan?"

"They were pleased with me, Mr. Crabbe. They knew I was efficient and they said so often."

"The Japanese prized efficiency, didn't they? It's no good, Jaganathan, you'll never understand the feeling we had in those days. We were on fire, ready to fight anyone. I don't think we could have done what you did. I may be wrong, but I don't think so. And now if the Communists took over here you'd just be the same. Anything for a bit of personal power. You make me sick."

"Mr. Crabbe, I will not stand for such words in my house. You shall go now."

"Oh, I'll go. But if you want a fight, Jaganathan, you can bloody well have one. I can fight dirty too."

"I will not fight. I will do my duty. I will have those articles typed in many copies and I will give them to the staff. And they will see what you are, and you will get no more co-operation from them. And I shall call a meeting of the parents and they shall know too. You will have only trouble now, Crabbe, nothing but trouble."

Crabbe raised his eyebrows. This was the first time Jaganathan had ever addressed him without the conventional honorific. He grinned. "Kindly remember you are speaking to your headmaster, Mr. Jaganathan."

"You will not be that for long."

"Long enough, Mr. Jaganathan." Crabbe picked his way delicately through a writhing pattern of children and reached the door. There the dog cursed him again. He cursed back this time. Startled, the dog retreated to the sugar-box which was its kennel. A black baby stared, sucking its thumb.

Crabbe, as he drove slowly back to his house, thought not of the declaration of war with Jaganathan, but of his own youth, disclosed so unexpectedly in those childish pages that smelt of the apple-loft. His heart jumped again with the shock of her memory leaping out at him from a pompous and ill-informed article. He saw her, smelt her, felt the dark curls above the white neck, held her. He hardly noticed the Jaguar drawing up on the other side of the palm-fringed road. It was Hardman, and with him was Father Laforgue. Both were solemn. The priest gave no greeting, staring straight ahead, holding something with care as if fearful of spilling it.

"I wanted to see you," said Crabbe. "I've got a bloody big bone to pick."

"Not now." Hardman whispered. "This is serious."

"This is serious, too. What the hell are you whispering for?"

"Be quiet. Can't you see what he's carrying? Where does Mahalingam live?"

"Mahalingam?"

"You know," Hardman was impatient. "That teacher who's ill. He's dying now. He wants to make his peace. He sent for Georges."

"Dying? Nobody told me; nobody tells me anything."

"Quick. Where does he live?"

"In the new married quarters. Round by the water-works."

"Take us there. Quick. There's no time to lose."

"Dying? Nobody ever told me." Crabbe reversed his car on to a shallow dune at the road's side, set his direction once more away from home. "He's a Muslim, isn't he?"

"He was. Hurry up. We may be too late."

Crabbe had never met Mahalingam and he suddenly felt ashamed of the fact. He knew where he lived, for he addressed a monthly pay cheque to him. He did not even know what disease he was suffering from. That was bad. Bad headmastership. He sped down the main road, the Jaguar purring after him, turned right by a decayed coconut plantation, turned left by the water-works, at length came to a block of bright new buildings. Where Mahalingam lived, or was dying, was evident from a ghoulish knot of people standing outside an open door, waiting.

"I had better go in alone," said Father Laforgue. He whispered too, aware that, despite the wide hot blue air and the noise of children, he carried with him the

Eucharist, core and focus of a silence of worshippers. He went in, Malays stepping back awkwardly, half resentfully, half fearful of magic they did not know. The white *padre* was going to kill Mahalingam, but that, it seemed, was what Mahalingam wanted. The wife, sullen-eyed, followed Father Laforgue into the house.

"There's going to be a hell of a row about this," said Hardman, seated at his wheel. "I hope nobody's going to talk too much. The authorities will come down on poor old Georges like a ton of bricks."

"I'd no idea he was dying." Crabbe was almost apologising to Hardman. Suddenly he changed his tone to the truculent, remembering other business. "What have you been saying to Jaganathan?"

"Saying? What do you mean? Who is Jaganathan?"

"You know damn well who Jaganathan is. You've been talking to him, haven't you? About me."

"Jaganathan? Is that your Tamil friend? Teacher at the school?"

"Oh, come off it. You know who he is. You've been telling him about my supposed Communist sympathies, haven't you? There's no point in denying it. What I want to know is, why? What in God's name have you got against me?"

"Let's get this straight, Victor. Who's been telling you all this?"

"Jaganathan himself. He said there was somebody else present when you told him. What exactly have you been saying to him?"

"But, honestly, Victor, I just can't think of a time when I ever spoke to the man. I don't think I've even met him." Hardman's white face was screwed up in what looked like honest bewilderment.

"What have you got against me? That's all I want to know. What harm have I ever done you?"

"But I don't see when I could have met him. I'm genuinely trying to think back. . . ."

"Not after that business with Ah Wing? You won't have to do much thinking back. I put it to you, as you lawyers say, that, for some reason best known to yourself, you got in touch with Jaganathan and informed him that I was sending food supplies to the Communists. Isn't that it?"

"Good God, man." Hardman looked shocked. "Do you honestly think I'd do that?"

"Well, what put the idea into his head? He's even gone to the trouble of getting old copies of the university magazine from Singapore. He's going to circulate some of the articles I wrote. He's going to raise a very unpleasant kind of hell. And it's you who started him off."

"Oh, God," said Hardman. "What a stupid thing. I remember now, I did meet him. I talked to him for about five minutes at the Istana. It was the Sultan's birthday. I said there was no harm in intellectual Communism. I said that, in our day, most young men were theoretical Communists. I must have instanced you as an example. I probably said that even you had been an intellectual Communist."

"Well, you've let me in for a hell of a lot of trouble."

"But he can't do anything. I mean, you wrote those articles ages ago, when people thought very differently . . ."

"I wish to God you'd keep your big mouth shut in future. Don't you see, people here aren't going to think in terms of phases. As far as they're concerned, what I believed when I was twenty I still believe. Time stands still in the East. They've got a lovely stick to beat another white oppressor with now. I suppose that's what you want.

You told me yourself you're no longer a white man."

"Look here, Victor, have a bit of sense. Nobody can do anything. The people in Government would just laugh. So would the police, for that matter."

"I know, I know. But that doesn't mean that I'm not going to have trouble here. God knows it's hard enough to do this job, without strikes and broken windows and slashed tyres and, probably, axes. Don't you see what you've done, you bloody idiot? You've just about ruined my career."

"Oh, come, that's going a bit far . . ."

"That's what you want, isn't it? You want me out of the way. You don't want me here laughing at the bloody mess you've made of your own career. That's it, isn't it? You don't want faces out of the past . . ."

"Look here, you're talking sheer damned nonsense. . . ."

Father Laforgue came to the door, stern, rebuking them with an upheld finger. They became aware also that the Malays, mild, interested, concerned, were watching, their mouths open.

"This is just a little undignified, isn't it?" said Hardman. "Rowing when there's a death going on in there. If you want to talk to me please come to my office. I don't like brawling in the streets."

"Oh, go to . . ." Crabbe shut his mouth on the obscenity, got into his car, started it viciously, and drove off, thinking: 'Three quarrels in twelve hours. It isn't right, it isn't like me; the tropics are getting me down; but I didn't start it all. What gets into other people?' Hardman, colour in his cheeks, lit a cigarette, trembled doing it, waited, watching the Abelard corner clumsily. When Father Laforgue came out he looked pleased.

"I think it is quite possible he will recover. Extreme

Unction often restores health. I often saw it in China. It is like a medicine."

"Yes." Hardman put the car into gear, drove away slowly.

"I think these people will be quiet about it. The wife was impressed, in spite of herself. They were quite amazed when he cheered up so visibly."

"Really?"

"One could make many converts here. I am sure of that. But Islam is so repressive. There is no freedom of conscience. It is very like Calvinism."

"I suppose it is."

"Drop me outside the town. I can pick up a trishaw. We must not be seen together. We do not want any trouble."

"No."

"What is the matter with you, Rupert? You are not saying very much." Father Laforgue chuckled. "I think I understand. I think you have had an embarrassing experience."

"Oh?"

"It is not easy to throw things over, just like that. You still believe, you see. It was like meeting a woman you think you no longer love. But your heart beats fast, just the same. And your mouth becomes very dry. I know nothing of such experiences, but I can well imagine what it is like. I am happier than you are, much happier. You can drop me here."

Father Laforgue stood by the roadside, vainly waiting for a trishaw to cruise by. But it was the Sabbath, and most men were going to the mosque. Hardman drove home, hearing several times on his way the thin wail of the muezzin calling the faithful to prayer.

13

The thinnest of shavings of silver, the new moon was sighted. Cannons sounded, the fasting month began. In the hot daytime sleep wrapped the town, servants and workmen drooped. Everywhere the air was loud with hawking and spitting, for even to swallow saliva was an infraction of the law. Only at nightfall came animation, as the fast was broken with brittle cakes and deep draughts of water. Then came the rice and the burning sauces, drum-beats, old men gathering to read the Koran. In the middle of the night the lights came on again, the last meal swallowed against time, and then, in pitch dark, the booming of the cannon, the first spitting of the long, dry stomach-rumbling day.

Now came the end of Hardman's long honeymoon. The silk girls bringing sherbet had gone, the beds i' the East were no longer soft. The khaki police scoured the town in the name of the Prophet and found easy prey in Hardman. On the third day of the fast he absently lit a cigarette on Jalan Laksamana, was apprehended by two bony constables and carried off to the Chief Kathi.

"You can no longer claim the privilelge of the white man. You are to us no longer a white man but a son of Islam. It is breaking the fast, contrary to the law, to smoke a cigarette. It is, moreover, foolishness to do so in public. Fined ten dollars."

"But smoking isn't the same as eating. I mean, the smoke goes into the lungs, not the stomach."

"Nothing must pass your lips during the hours of fasting." The Kathi was a gentle old man but hard as a rock. "Fined ten dollars."

It was now that Hardman began to feel himself cut off completely from his own kind. He might before have deplored the fact that Islam left so little to the individual conscience, but his objections had been academic, because the teeth of Islam had not yet touched him. Now he was made to feel like a schoolboy chewing toffee in class. He saw the other Europeans eating publicly during the daytime, swallowing beer in *kedais*, come roistering out of the Club. The adolescent drinking-parties at lunch-time now seemed strangely adult. Even around the club the police hovered: he was such easy prey, desirable prey too, because he was still a white man. He was getting the worst of both worlds.

Cut off from Crabbe, he was also cut off from Georges Laforgue. That safe meeting place was denied him now. And in his home tempers grew ever more ragged with thirst and hunger. But he dreaded the breaking of the fast too, for Normah's advances became ritualistic and regular. Because all fleshly enjoyments were banished during the day, it became almost a religious duty for her to drag him to bed shortly after the evening gun was shot off. He became thinner, paler, more nervous, and was obsessed by a kind of claustrophobia, often waking at night in a frightful dream of smothering.

And there was no release. He could no longer look at himself from the outside, for there was no one to talk to now. He was genuinely drifting away from the West, and the fancy dress of Islam began to feel like his ordinary clothes. Suffocated, one day he drove twenty miles to a Government Rest House that stood by a ferry on the banks of the Sungai Dahaga. There he ordered beer from the adenoidal Chinese manager and drank the afternoon away, greedily swilling bottle after bottle, feeling gradually his adulthood return. For some reason he began to scribble *pensées* in his pocket diary:

"*The Arabian Nights* is essentially a book for boys."

"The Koran is obviously the work of an illiterate."

"Proclaiming the oneness of God is like proclaiming the wetness of water."

"I shall go mad."

He was not paying his way. His practice was not flourishing. He was a kept man. He drove back singing Parry's 'Jerusalem', entering the town as the gun was fired. He had a feeling that the police would stop him to smell his breath, that probably already the authorities had learnt of his afternoon's debauch, but to hell with the lot of them. He was civilised, adult. He was a barrister, a scholar, a cosmopolitan. He had drunk wine in Italy, eaten octopus by the Middle Sea, seen castles in Germany, talked with poets in Soho. He enclosed these people here, he was bigger than they.

As he approached the house he remembered that it was not his but his wife's. He felt fear stir through the thick beery euphoria. He dared not go home. Impulsively he drove to the Club—was he not entitled to? The fasting day was over; he was breaking no law—and soaked whisky with a sweat-shirted, hairy-kneed gang of planters in for the day.

At eleven o'clock one planter said: "Come back to dinner."

"Dinner? Now?"

"A few drinks first. Then dinner. Never have dinner

before midnight." He swayed happily on his bar-stool.

"Love to," said Hardman. He steadied himself against the billiard-table.

"Stay the night if you like. Plenty of beds. Everybody come and spend the night."

"Yes," said Hardman. "Spend the night. Called away on a case. Forgot to inform the wife. Yes." He felt safe. The protecting flag fluttered above, proud in the hostile air. Sanctuary. He was with his own kind.

It is unwise ever to feel safe. Bombs have been hurled into Residencies. 'Che Normah had every right to enter the Club of which her husband was a full member.

She would not let him drive back. The car, her car, could stay the night outside the Club. She had kept her trishaw waiting. They were pedalled slowly back, wedged together, and 'Che Normah said little, for she could afford self-control. In the house the army attacked, knives flew at him, a transfixed Saint Sebastian. A thousand voices seemed to fill the hundred-watt-lit room. It was superb, it was the glory of God in a tropical storm, it was mountains and jungles, fire and avalanches. She was Cassandra, Medea, harpies and furies. Red-hot Malay flowed like steel from a furnace. Hardman was pinned by her eyes, buoyed up by her cosmic energy, a scrap of paper in a maelstrom of hot air.

Then he broke. He screeched an Arabic word. In his whisky-confused mind it seemed an exorciser's charm, but it was a term that had lodged, like a fragment of food in a tooth, from the grind of his legal reading. It was the Islamic formula of divorce.

"*Talak!*"

She stopped, amazed, shocked, incredulous, as if hearing a child utter a dirty word.

"*Talak!*"

"That is twice," she said. "It has to be three times." She looked at him, fascinated, as though he were cutting his cheek with a razor-blade.

"*Talak!*"

"That is three times," she said. "That is divorce." Then, calm, as though well-satisfied, she sat down and took a cigarette. She said, in English, "You are silly boy." Then she followed up in good clear slow Malay, "You must not say that. It is very dangerous."

Hardman danced up and down, sweating violently, incoherent, croaking obscenities, ending with a refrain like the end of an Upanishad.

"Bitch! Bitch! Bitch!"

"You must never, never say that again. You must not try to divorce me. One man tried it before. It is very, very dangerous for you to say that." She looked at him, her eyes softened, almost indulgently. "You see, it would be the end of you." She had not even seemed to hear the flow of execration. She held the Arabic word like a weapon wrested from a naughty child, a weapon more deadly than the child knows. One is too shocked to think that a child can get such a weapon to be cross with the child; one even feels a paradoxical respect for the child, seeing that a child can be dangerous. The word was magical enough; it had quietened the devils. But Normah's cigarette-smoking calm, her softer, more thoughtful eyes, her slow words were deadlier than any devils. Hardman's foodless day, his full stomach of beer and whisky began to send queasy messages. The sweat was all over his body.

"Have you eaten?" said Normah. He shook his head. "There is cold curry." He shook his head again. "You must eat. You will be ill."

"Don't want to eat." He was spent. He sat on the floor, his forehead against the cool wall, eyes closed, but aware that she was appraising him as though he were a choice exhibit at the slave-market.

"Come to bed, then."

"Don't want to come to bed."

"Ruperet," she said, honey in her mouth, as she undressed him with cool brown fingers, "you are not to say things like that again. It can be very bad for you if you say things like that. I will forget that you said it and you will forget that you said it. We will say no more about it. We shall be very, very happy together and love each other. Now you will come to bed."

He was led off, white nakedness, tottering, thin with bird's bones, the cosmopolitan, the scholar, the man who enclosed these people. He passed out quickly. The beds i' the East are soft.

14

"It's just pouring out of me," said Anne Talbot. "They talk about love in the tropics. It's just adding heat to heat." She lay back exhausted on the hard single bed. "A temperate zone. Winter. Frost on the window. And when you get into the bed first you shiver. That's for me."

"It *is* hot tonight," said Crabbe. He wiped himself all over with a bed-sheet. "A pity there's no fan."

"No fan, no bath, no civilised lavatory. Hawking and spitting on the stairs. Whatever made you choose this place?"

"Secrecy. Nobody cares here. Nobody knows." Outside in the narrow street, British troops, repressed after their jungle stints, roared with drink, spilling long-saved dollars. Later they would fight, pass out, or pant in venery. From below, in the hotel bar, the noise of the juke-box filtered up. Crabbe looked out, rubbing sweat from his back. "We couldn't very well stay at any of the reputable places. Malaya's only a parish."

"Nine o'clock," said Anne Talbot, peering at her watch on the table, flopping again on to the soaked pillow. "You choose the absurdest times. Too early for sleep, too late to get dressed again."

"I choose?" He sat beside her.

"You're developing a paunch. Just like Herbert, but not quite as big. But, then, you're younger. And you smell."

She turned over on to her face. Her voice came muffled. "You smell of man."

"That's the tropics again. We all smell in the tropics. And Herbert, you'll remember, smells of more than himself. Onions and cheese and cocoa."

"Oh, shut up about Herbert."

The small room looked squalid, clothes strewn about, two empty glasses, a plate on which ants crawled. From next door a portable radio oscillated, swelled up in a burst of Hindustani, modulated to a chatter of Chinese. The hundred-watt bulb, naked, beat down warm on their nakedness.

"The Muddy Estuary," said Crabbe. "Or, as Jean Cocteau called it, *Kouala L'impure*. Listen to that." Howls and a smash of glass came from the street below. "Come on, we'll go out. We'll have a drink somewhere."

"Where? We can't go to the Club, we can't go to the Harlequin. The town's full of conferring headmasters. They all know us. Certainly, they all know me."

"Yes." There actually was a headmasters' conference. That palliated a little the sense of guilt. And Anne was, so Talbot believed, staying with a woman friend who was in Radio Malaya.

"Come on, we'll go somewhere." Crabbe wanted to get out of the sweating airless room with its tortured grey sheets.

They dressed. Applying lipstick, Anne said, "Tell me. When you talk about love, is that just the voice of tumescence?"

"Partly."

"Because I've got to get out. I'm not going to live with him any longer. He not only eats but drinks as well. Then he becomes all hairy arms. The only room I can lock

159

myself in is the lavatory. You can't spend the rest of your life in the lavatory."

"When did this happen?"

"It often happens. It happened the night before I left."

"Poor darling," said Crabbe. He kissed her left ear. She looked at him, not too warmly, in the mirror.

"The point is," she said, "what are you going to do about it?"

"What am I going to do?"

"Yes, dear. You have a certain responsibility towards me, you know." Crabbe, in tight tie and palm-beach suit, sat on the unused bed and scooped sweat off his forehead. "What do you want me to do?" he asked.

"The time will come when he'll have to divorce me. He knows that. He can't put it off indefinitely. When he's a big enough laughing-stock he'll do something. He's got his precious career to think about."

"And where do I come in?"

She turned from the mirror, reintegrated, demure, after her self-indulgence of the previous hour. "You can send Fenella home," she said. "She's always moaning about wanting to go home."

"She won't go home without me."

"She'll go home soon enough. She'll go home for good."

"You want me to get a divorce? Is that it?"

"You please yourself about that. You've certainly got ample grounds."

"She says that the Abang hasn't done anything wrong. She says he just worships her from afar. Anyway, what do you want?"

"I want to get away from Herbert."

"You don't have to stay with him, you know. You can always get out."

"How? Where do I go? What do I use for money? I can't even get the fare home unless he authorises it."

Crabbe lit a cigarette, looked at her through the smoke. "I still don't see where I come in. Do you want us to be married?"

"No. I'll never marry again. I want to be free. Give me one of those." He lit her cigarette.

"I see. You just want to use me, is that it? You want me to help create so big a scandal that he'll let you go. And then what do you do?"

"I stay with you."

Crabbe gazed in astonishment at the demure boy-gangster's face. "And what exactly happens to *my* precious career?"

"You haven't got one. Not here, anyway. You've left it all too late. When you've finished this tour you won't come back. Unless you accept a contract with the Government. If you stay in the Oversea Civil Service you'll have to go somewhere else. Borneo, Hong Kong . . . There aren't many places left, are there? But Herbert will probably see his time out."

"How do you know all this?"

"Oh, information's coming through. They want the white men out quickly."

"So it's all been in vain," said Crabbe, gazing at the bare floor. "It's too late." Was it worth fighting Jaganathan? Hardman was right: the twilight was here, the twilight in which man can do some work, but unhandily. Not enough light, bats fly into your eyes, mosquitoes bite. If you loved, your love was rarely returned. Malaya didn't want him.

"Be honest, Victor," she said. "You don't want marriage. You're like me. You want love with the door open. I could make you happy for as long as you wanted. Or as long as I wanted."

"There was a time when I was really married. I think it only happens once."

"You were lucky. Listen, Victor." She sat beside him. "I've been good. Haven't I? Really good. Nobody knows about us. Not a soul. I've been clever."

"Fenella suspects something."

"Not much. And I've got some decency. I don't flaunt things. And we're being careful here, aren't we? All too damn careful. But I do care for you, you see, I care for you quite a lot."

"I care for you, too," he said lamely, putting a hot hand on her cool one. She drew it away, concerned only with what she was saying.

"If you care for me, for God's sake don't let me suffer. We can be together till the end of your tour. You can save something. You can get me home. That's the least you can do. But I can't go on with him, I just can't. He's making me physically sick, just his being there, gorging and mouthing his filthy poetry, and then smelling of whisky and coming for me with his hairy arms." Somehow this did not sound like Talbot, the mild, yokel-locked, moon-faced, fat-boy-buttocked.

Crabbe sighed. "It's so difficult," he began.

"Difficult? How about my difficulties? You just don't begin to understand. You're ready enough to take me to bed, aren't you? You make enough noise about loving me. But when it comes to a real bit of help, you're just like the rest of them . . ."

"The rest of them?"

"The rest of them. All men. Selfish. Out for what they can get. Oh, come on, let's go for that drink."

They went down the narrow stairs, seeing on the bare treads odd dirty plates and bottles of soya sauce. The manager of the hotel stood at its entrance, sucking a toothpick, dressed in vest and underpants. He gave them no greeting. In the hot street Malay and Indian urchins called, *"Taksi, tuan?"* and begged for small coins. Troops lurched singing, and a fat Chinese prostitute spat loudly into the monsoon-drain. Anne and Crabbe walked to a drinking-shop outside which stood a posse of military police.

Smoke, shouting talk and loud metallic music hit them. Crabbe ordered beer. At the bar leaned a moustached plump-shouldered young man in an evening gown. Loud and sloppy-mouthed the troops sang, mindless of the whores who clung to them. A glass was smashed in a far corner.

"This is not quite my line," said Anne. "And we can't talk here." A reinforcement of fresh troops staggered in, one man soaked and dripping, his hair sticky with the chrism of poured beer, another with his pockets crammed with sauce-bottles. Above the partition of the alcove where Anne and Crabbe were sitting a wandering hand appeared. It groped and lighted on Anne's hair. She cried out, inaudible in the solid noise, and Crabbe touched the hand with his lighted cigarette. The hand disappeared back to its own world and was not seen again.

Half-way through their beer they saw the main fight start. It came into their view, segment after segment, like a groaning thudding wave, heralded by a piling-up of chairs and tables, flopping bottles and broken glass. The fight was an anthology of all the techniques—punching, kicking, jagged bottles into faces. A young wild-haired Tamil kicked high like a ballet dancer, a fair-haired New

Zealand private bit his opponent's ear. The wave broke at the juke-box which tottered in a flicker of coloured lights. The military police entered, and, under their cover, Crabbe and Anne left.

They took a taxi to Campbell Road where, in the vast open-air eating-hell, they ordered beer, chicken soup and fried *mee*.

"You know," said Anne, "the whole thing's just turning out to be sordid. I didn't expect it to be like this at all. And we could have so good a time. You know that."

Crabbe took her hand. "We'll think about it," he said. The gloom of the twilight was settling on him. Did anything matter any more? Perhaps the days of circumspection were over. Perhaps Anne really understood him. Perhaps what she wanted he wanted too.

"Oh, God," said Anne. "We're back in Kenching. Look who's over there."

At a small table, bowing to them, was Father Laforgue. He was in his surgical white, smiling, happy with a crowd of animated Chinese.

"But what on earth's he doing here?" wondered Crabbe. "He can't afford any holidays."

"Perhaps there's an ecclesiastical conference as well," said Anne.

Father Laforgue came over. He shook hands and spoke rapid French.

"A drink, Father?"

He shook his head. *"Merci."*

"What are you doing in this galley?"

"I am no longer in Dahaga," said Father Laforgue. "I have been ejected."

"Slower, slower, please."

"They have thrown me out." He spoke without bitterness. "You will remember when this teacher of yours was dying. He was not so ill as he thought. Moreover, the sacrament of Extreme Unction often has the power to restore health when God sees it to be expedient. This may well have happened. And, to show his gratitude, he has denounced me to the Islamic authorities. Or. rather, I think it was his wife who did this. Our good friend Rupert is in great trouble also. His wife was very annoyed to learn that Rupert had taken me to Mahalingam's house in his car. Or, rather, she says it is her car. She is having one of their holy men to come and exorcise it." Father Laforgue smiled. "In some ways it is very amusing, of course. But I am very sorry for Rupert. He is having great trouble with the authorities now, and his wife has been most angry with him. All this because we try to help a man who is dying."

"When did this happen?" asked Crabbe.

"The day before yesterday I was given my notice to quit. I was given only twenty-four hours. Some of my Chinese friends raised the money for my air passage and they are arranging to send on my books. I reported here yesterday and I now await instructions." He continued to smile. "I am not sorry for myself. Here I have met many Chinese, far more than in Dahaga. And there is a Chinese schoolmaster here who is writing a book on Chinese philosophy. But it is poor Rupert I am thinking about. Although, in a way, it is a kind of judgement on him. God is not mocked."

"Do have a drink."

"No. If you will excuse me, I will return to my friends. We are to have some shark's fin soup. On the east coast you cannot get good shark's fin soup. Here you can. And then we are to go to a midnight showing of a Chinese film. You see, there is plenty to do here."

"Your parish will miss you," said Crabbe.

"My parish. Yes, my parish." Father Laforgue shrugged his shoulders. "They will get somebody else." Candidly he added, "Somebody better. Good-night, Mr. Crabbe. Good-night, Mrs. Crabbe." He had no longer much of a memory for European faces.

Sweating again that night in the stifling room, Crabbe felt a sort of love well up for Anne. It was the sort of love she seemed to want. A love with the door open, she had said. For him there had only been one time when he had wanted the door locked and bolted, enclosing a love that must never escape. That door was still locked and bolted, but now he was on the outside, only in sleep hammering vainly to be let in again.

The day before the end of the conference he returned to the hotel at midday. Anne was seated at the small bar, drinking, talking quietly but earnestly with a man in uniform. The only other occupant of the room was a dishevelled soldier, drinking steadily, spilling drink among screwed-up dollar bills which were scattered over the table. He drooled incessantly, alternately moaning and cursing in a low somniloquist's voice. Anne turned as Crabbe entered, feigning surprise. Crabbe then saw that the man in uniform was Bannon-Fraser.

"Victor," she cried. "What are you doing in K.L.?"

He played up. Good girl, she was protecting his reputation.

"It's a small world," said Bannon-Fraser. "I'm on a course here. Damn silly to send me on a course just when my contract's coming to an end. But typical, I suppose."

"Are they renewing your contract?" asked Crabbe. Behind them, the forlorn soldier suddenly cursed loud and clear.

"Really," said Anne.

"They got him! They got him, the bastards! Best bloody pal a man ever had."

"No, they're not," said Bannon-Fraser. "In spite of the fact that the Emergency's still in full swing. Still, I'm not worrying. I've got myself fixed up with a job in Singapore. With a Chinese transport firm. I've nothing to go back home for, and I like Singapore. The pay's good, too."

"Congratulations," said Crabbe. He sipped the gin Bannnon-Fraser had bought for him. "What are you doing here?" he said to Anne. He enjoyed these harmless charades.

"Seeing a specialist. It's my old trouble again." She turned innocent eyes on him. "I can't sleep at nights with it."

"I didn't know you frequented dives like this."

"Well, I don't normally. But I was looking at the shops and felt thirsty and this place looked reasonably quiet. And I was just sipping a harmless orange squash when Jock walked in. As he says, it's a small world." Crabbe did not smile back. Had this been arranged? The barboy tapped him on the arm and gave him some letters. Forwarded bills, by the look of them.

"Yes, I'm staying here," said Crabbe. "How the poor live."

"But how frightful," said Anne. "It's so squalid. The sort of place people might go for a week-end."

"Yes," said Crabbe. "That sort of place." He gazed at her levelly. *"Nostalgie de la boue* on my part."

"I've got to lunch with a chap at the Selangor Club," said Bannon-Fraser. "I'm sorry to shoot off like this. Can I give you a lift, Anne? You didn't tell me where you were staying, by the way."

"With a friend."

"Have a drink!" called the soldier. "Best bloody pal a man ever had."

"Well, can I take you there or anything? Or perhaps Crabbe wants to give you lunch."

"Victor has his reputation to think of," said Anne. "He can't be seen lunching with the wife of his superior officer."

"My reputation can take care of itself," said Crabbe. "If yours can. I should be honoured if you would lunch with me."

"Toffy-nosed bastards!" mumbled the soldier. "Won't have a drink."

Bannon-Fraser gave a smooth demonstration of man-management. "Sorry, old chap," he said. "We can't stay. Some other time. And do watch your language in front of a lady, there's a good chap."

"They killed him, I tell you. Those bastards killed him."

"I know, and they've nearly killed me. Well, I've got to be going," said Bannon-Fraser. "Could we all meet, do you think, tonight? Do the town and all the rest of it. Safety in numbers." He turned on to Anne an advertisement-smile, put on his cap, looking, all clichés of handsomeness, every inch a Home Guard officer.

"That would be nice," said Anne.

"Look here," said Crabbe. "We'll come too. That is, if you'd like to," he added, to Anne. "I believe the food's rather good at the Selangor Club. You could give us a lift," he said to Bannon-Fraser.

"I don't particularly want any lunch," said Anne. "I rarely eat it."

"If you'll excuse me," said Bannon-Fraser. "Let's meet at the Harlequin about eight. Will that be all right?" Smiling, young, muscular, paunchless, probably odourless, he went. The soldier called after him:

"Stuck-up bastard."

"Well," said Crabbe. "Was this all aranged?"

"Was what arranged?"

"You knew he was here, didn't you? Knew he was in K.L.?"

"I'd heard vaguely that he was on a course, yes."

"And it's starting all over again, isn't it?"

"Oh, Victor." She fingered his wrist. "That was all over a long time ago."

"Now you're just friends."

"Oh, that is possible, you know."

"Come and sit down here, lady," said the soldier. "Have a drink with me."

"Fancy you being jealous," she said. "Remember what you were always saying?"

"What?"

"That you didn't want to start anything."

The soldier now lurched towards the bar, put an arm round each of them and looked blearily into their faces. He smelt of everything the bar stocked, his strawy hair was wild, and he had splashed beer over his jungle-green. "They killed him," he said. "He was ambushed. That's why I'm getting pissed, see? You get pissed with me," he invited.

"Please stop pawing me," said Anne sharply. "Victor, tell him to go away."

"Go away," said Crabbe.

"Found his body, they did, full of holes, see? That's why I'm . . ."

Anne wrenched herself away and went towards the door. Crabbe followed. The white-hot light of the street hit them, noise of cars, bicycles, brown urchins.

"That was rather unfortunate," he said.

"Oh, it's so sordid, sordid. I shan't go back there. I shall go somewhere else."

"It won't be for much longer."

"No, it won't."

"Please, Anne." Crabbe tried to take her arm. "Don't be angry."

She slowed her walk. "I'm not angry. I'm just tired, that's all. I'm not having much of a life. And think what I've got to go back to."

"That won't be for long, either."

"I wonder."

That night they did the town. It was all very decorous. They drank in the bars of reputable hotels, Crabbe and Bannon-Fraser neck-tied and jacketed, spilling, among other members of their race and class, their colonial bromides on the conditioned air, Bannon-Fraser, handsome, vacuous, neatly locked with Anne on the small dance-floors, telling innocent jokes at the bar, greeting friends with a warm chubby laugh. At midnight they left the air-conditioned dream-world and entered the oven of the street.

"I'll drop you first, shall I, Crabbe?" Here it was, then.

"Yes, do that."

Outside the hotel in the rough singing drunken street, the Sikh watchman asleep on his *charpoy*, the manager standing indifferent, sucking his tooth-pick, Crabbe said good-night.

"Good-night, Victor," said Anne, looking up from the front passenger seat.

"Good-night, old boy," said Bannon-Fraser. "It was a nice evening."

15

While Crabbe was packing his bags Anne came to collect hers.

"I'll pay my own bill, Victor. That's only fair."

"No, we came as a married couple. We'll end that way. What are you going to do?"

"We're going to Singapore."

"But his contract hasn't finished yet."

"There's only a month to go. He thinks they'll let him spend it here, doing some sort of office work."

"And where are you going to stay?"

She smiled. "Ah, that would be telling. I don't want Herbert following me, begging me to come back, revelling in a nice sweaty scene."

"Do you honestly think I'd tell him?"

"You might, dear. I don't trust men."

"Except Bannon-Fraser?"

"I don't even trust him. But trustworthiness isn't everything."

"Have I to tell Herbert anything at all?"

"No. I'm going to write. Look, you're not feeling bitter, are you?"

"Not particularly. You've always been pretty honest."

"I've tried to be. What time's your plane?"

"One o'clock."

"You'd better kiss me good-bye. You still mean a great deal to me, Victor."

"I'll get your luggage taken downstairs."

"No, just go. I'll see to all that."

"Good-bye, then." He kissed her lightly. As he opened the door she called after him:

"Victor! What are *you* going to do?"

"Oh, I shall just carry on. I suppose I'd better try being a good husband. There's a better chance of that now."

"Can you be a good husband?"

"I once had the gift. I suppose I can find it again."

"That's not really likely to happen, is it?"

Crabbe did not answer. "Good-bye, Anne," he said. "I hope you'll be happy."

Leaning back in his armchair high above the jungle, lulled by the engine-noises, Crabbe tried to take stock of himself. He felt very much alone. Malaya did not want him. The romantic dream he had entertained, the dream that had driven Raffles to early death, was no longer appropriate to an age in which sleep was impossible. The whole East was awake, building dams and canals, power-houses and car factories, forming committees, drawing up constitutions, having selected from the West the few tricks it could understand and use. The age of Raffles was also the age of Keats and Shelley, the East attractively misty, apt for the muffled clang of the romantic image—Cathay all golden dragons, Japan the edge of the world. Liberalism, itself a romantic dream, had long gone under, and there was no longer any room for the individual, there was nothing now that any one man could build. Crabbe remembered some lines from an unfinished sonnet of Hopkins, one that Fenella had once quoted to him:

Or what is else? There is your world within.
There rid the dragons, root out there the sin.
Your will is law in that small commonweal. . . .

The time had come to start thinking about his private
life. Perhaps there were really two kinds of marriage, both
equally valid: the one that was pure inspiration, the poem
come unbidden; the one that had to be built, laboriously,
with pain and self-abasement, deliberate engineering,
sweat and broken nails. He saw his unkindness to Fenella,
the demon that urged him on to believe that it was all a
mistake, that she, in some way, was the usurper. One could
not spend one's life being loyal to the dead. That was
romanticism of the worst sort. In Indonesia the jungle had
been cleared and rice planted. It was time he cleared the
romantic jungle in which he wanted to lurk, acknowledged
that life was striving not dreaming, and planted the seeds
of a viable relationship between his wife and himself.

He reached Kenching in the early evening. To his surprise he found that Talbot had come to meet him. As the
plane taxied, he saw the stumpy figure, greying tow hair,
spectacles, plump legs in running shorts, striding up and
down the length of his parked car. Alighted, Crabbe
greeted him with false and guilty cheerfulness. Talbot was
grim.

"Come on," he said. "I'm taking you home. I want to
talk to you."

"Oh, what's happened? Is it Jaganathan again?"

Talbot started the engine, clumsily put it into gear.
"You know damn well it's not that I want to talk about.
It's about you and my wife."

"Yes?" Crabbe swallowed hard.

"You've been carrying on with her in K.L., haven't you?

174

I might have known. Bloody fool that I was. I wouldn't have thought of it if your wife hadn't put the idea into my head."

"My wife?"

"Yes. And then this chap Hardman sees your wife in the town and says that he thought she was in K.L. with you, because that French priest sent him a post-card saying that he'd met you both, and then she put two and two together. For Christ's sake, how long has this been happening?" He drove somewhat crookedly down the main road.

"Herbert, will you wait? Wait just a couple of days."

"She's out, she's finished. You can bloody well have her, because I won't. I didn't expect you to think about me, but you might have thought about your wife. As though she isn't having enough trouble."

"What sort of trouble?"

"Oh, she'll tell you. Perhaps she won't. I don't think she wants to speak to you again. I don't bloody well blame her."

"Herbert, please listen."

"There's nothing more to say. The damage has been done. Bloody fool I must look to the people in K.L."

"Herbert, listen. I might as well tell you, because you'll find out soon enough. She's writing to you."

"Writing? What about?"

"Do you remember a man called Bannon-Fraser?"

Talbot stopped the car, very deliberately, by the side of the road.

"Bannon-Fraser? He's still here, isn't he?"

"He went on a course to K.L. I met him there. I met him there with Anne. They're going off together."

Talbot thought for a moment and said, "You needn't

try and get out of it that way. You needn't try to put it all on to somebody else."

"But it's true. She's writing to tell you. He's getting a job in Singapore. She says they're going to live together."

"Where are they now? By Christ, if I find them both . . ." Talbot looked at Crabbe sternly. "How do I know you're telling me the truth?"

"You'll soon know. She's sending you a letter."

"How do you know all this? Are you in on it, too? By Christ, when I find them, I'll bloody well . . . Where are they? Where are they living?"

A Malay labourer paused on his way home from work. He gazed open-mouthed into the car, much struck by Talbot's agitation. Crabbe waved him away.

"I don't know. She refused to tell me."

"I'll find them. I'll scour the whole damned town. This is the end of him. This is the end of both of them."

"It's not worth it, Herbert. You can't do anything."

"Do anything? I'll drag them out. I'll tell the whole damned Federation about it." He gripped the steering-wheel hard, lowered his forehead on to the nub as if to cool it. Then he raised his eyes and said, "What sort of a woman is she? Is she a prostitute? First she's with you, then she's with this other swine. I just don't know her. I just don't know anything."

"We had a meal together one evening. That's all."

Talbot started to sob, though his eyes remained dry.

"Don't you think it's better this way?" said Crabbe. "You know it's never worked. Be honest, has it? I knew the first day I met you both that it would never work." He patted comfortingly the fat shaking shoulder.

"She was all I had," cried Talbot. "I gave her everything."

"There's plenty for you still," said Crabbe. "There's your work, there's your poetry. Great poetry's made out of great sorrow, you know."

"Great sorrow," sobbed Talbot. "I'll never write again."

"Look," said Crabbe, "go to my house. Tell Fenella all about it. She'll understand. She'll be sympathetic. You're both poets, remember. You can drop me at the school. I left my car in the school garage—safer there with a care-taker on the spot. I'll pick it up and come round in about half an hour, then we can have a meal together."

"Yes," said Talbot, calmer now. "One's got to eat. One's got to carry on." Then, almost cheerful, he said, "You haven't got a car now."

"What do you mean?"

"Nothing left of it. Just a mass of old iron. There's been a fire, you know. Somebody burnt the garage down. And the boys' lavatory's gone as well."

"Jaganathan."

"Oh, no, I don't think so. Jaganathan's been away. In Malacca, I think. But it was a hell of a fire. Hell of a job putting it out."

"When did it happen? Why didn't somebody let me know?"

"Only a couple of days ago. It hardly seemed worth while to write to you. And Fenella's been so upset."

"About . . . ?"

"Yes, about that." In sudden Ercles vein, Talbot cried, "When I find the pair of them, I'll kill them both. I will. They've ruined me, made me look the biggest bloody fool . . ."

Thank God he'd remembered to renew the insurance. 'And now,' thought Crabbe, with a sudden lifting of spirits, 'the Abang can have it. I've kept him waiting long enough. He shall have it, any time he likes.' "Come on," he said to Talbot, "let's go home."

Talbot needed no persuading to enter the house first. He raged in, loud and bitter about Anne's treachery, about what he would do to Bannon-Fraser. Crabbe held him in front, an umbrella against an expected squall, and soon Fenella had melted enough to accept a kiss of greeting. But she had had enough trouble. At dinner she spoke of it.

"One of the bedroom windows. A stone straight through it. And people keep shaking their fists. And then this fire at the school, and the car. It's been horrible. I stayed three nights at the Istana."

"At the Istana?"

"Yes. They gave me one of the guest-rooms. The Abang was very kind."

The new Malay cook brought in more potatoes for Talbot. A mass of carbohydrate induced a philosophical outlook, and Talbot, spreading thick butter on his bread, began to recite, his eyes moist behind their glasses:

"But loss, too, is at least a thing which, in the dark,
    We can hold, feeling a sharpness, knowing that a knife
    Is a double-edged weapon, for carving as well as killing.
    The knife in the abattoir is also the knife on the table,
    The corpse becomes meat, the dead stone heart the raw
    Stuff of the sculptor's art. . . ."

"Do have a little more beef," said Fenella. "I'm afraid the gravy's rather cold now, but there's Worcestershire sauce if you'd like it."

Talbot champed away, finally spooning in resignation with the tinned fruit salad, calm of mind reached with the last piece of cheese, all passion spent in the third drained coffee-cup. Patting his stomach, he said that he would now be getting along home. He had a poem to write.

"And I'm sorry I thought what I did, Victor. I should have known better."

"That's all right, Herbert."

Left alone, Fenella and Crabbe sat stiffly, embarrassed. Crabbe spoke first.

"I've had time to think. I've not been a very good husband, Fenella. Will you believe me when I say that I want to start again?"

"I can quite believe that you do. We obviously couldn't go on like that for ever."

"And I do love you. I see that quite clearly now."

"Do you?" She seemed cold still, withdrawn, sitting upright in the bamboo armchair. Then she got up, walked over to the glass-topped table that stood under a Paul Klee reproduction, and took a cigarette from the box there. Crabbe was aware of her grace, the gold beauty, and tried to force the name 'love' on the pity that rose in him.

"It may be too late, Victor," she said. "I'm not saying it is. It just may be."

"I don't think I understand."

"You were never very good at understanding me. You've never really tried. Curiously enough, I've been learning a lot about myself lately. I've been seeing things very clearly. For instance, I've discovered that I'm quite an attractive woman. That I'm also intelligent. That I've got quite a lot to give people."

"All that's perfectly true."

"But you've never told me. Never once. I'm not saying it's your fault. But there's only been one woman in your life. Be honest about it, Victor. You've always been comparing me with her. You've never been able to see me clearly."

"It was true. But you can't be ill all your life. I've been convalescing. I know what I want now. You must give me this chance, Fenella. I can be happy with you. I want you to be happy with me."

"Yes. I think you really mean that. It's curious that this should happen now."

"Curious?"

"Yes. Just when somebody else is telling me the same thing."

Crabbe started. "You don't mean . . . ?"

"Yes, Yusof's been telling me." Crabbe frowned, puzzled. "Yusof is the Abang. And he isn't what people think he is. He hasn't laid a hand on me. He hasn't even attempted . . ."

"Oh, Fenella," said Crabbe, "don't be so innocent. He'll wait, he'll lull you till it's time for him to pounce."

"No," said Fenella, "he won't do that. I'm quite sure. I think I know him quite well. You see, when we meet, we just talk. Sometimes in Malay, sometimes in English. I think I've cured him of that American accent. He sounds quite reasonable now. He tells me he's never really talked to a woman before, and I can believe him. Apparently, Islam doesn't approve of women talking."

"What do you talk about?"

"Oh, I'm really trying to teach him. He knows so little of life, really, especially *our* sort of life. And it's our sort of life he needs to learn about, because he won't be here much longer. He's been persuading me very strongly to go home. He says that when he goes to Europe—as he will, very soon—I could help him a great deal. He's not asking for anything, except my help."

"I see."

"So, Victor, it turns out that *I'm* really the teacher. Queer, isn't it? You come out here to bring the great gifts of the West, and you say you've failed, but *I've* not failed. I've certainly taught something."

"And so you really want to go home?"

"I don't know. Not yet, anyway. It still depends on you."

"I've told you, darling, I want to try. Things can be very different. And I'm going to need you more than I've ever needed anybody."

"I wonder."

Crabbe was about to speak, to renew his protestations, when the noise of a motor was heard drawing up outside the house. From it came the sound of a fat voice, singing in an unknown tongue.

"I forgot to tell you," said Fenella. "We have police protection now. The Abang arranged it himself. A rather old Sikh constable. I don't suppose he'd be much good in a crisis, but he seems to scare away our enemies, whoever they are."

"There's only one."

"No. You've failed, Victor. We're not wanted any more, any of us. It's all enemies from now on. God, that sounds melodramatic. But politics, of course, is all melodrama. Unbelievably crude."

"I'm getting resigned, you know. I heard a few things in Kuala Lumpur. We shan't be coming back, that's reasonably certain. But . . ."

"I know what you're going to say. Will I stay with you here until the time comes to pack up completely? That, as I've said, depends."

"Because 'going home' is a euphemism for . . ."

"You're not slow, Victor. I sometimes forget you can be quite bright. But you don't give me much of a chance, do you? 'Going home' means what you think it means. Either it works, this being together, or it doesn't. And if it doesn't . . . Well, I'm still young. And, as Yusof says, attractive. I'm entitled to a bit of life."

"Just what Anne says."

"Anne? Yes, I know about that, too. Nothing's easy to hide in a country like this. But I'm not blaming you any more. I understand now. And I pity . . ."

"Pity?" Crabbe looked up at her, still standing, with an expression of small surprise, eyes narrowed in a weak show of outrage.

"We'd better go to bed. To-morrow we'll go to the beach. It's a long time since I had a swim."

Kartar Singh gave jovial greeting from the veranda. In return, he was given beer. The Crabbes went to bed, leaving their guard to sing quietly to himself as he made his tour of the perimeter, ending up outside the bedroom itself, whence he heard no sound. The white man, as Kartar Singh knew, was cold. The white man had no red blood in his veins. This was the hour for the dancing of the springs, but from the two sundered beds came not even the sound of sleeping. Kartar Singh smiled fatly and happily resumed his round.

16

The driver of the trishaw reclined in the double wicker seat and watched them idly, picking his teeth. They had asked him to wait for an hour. One hour, two hours, three: it made no difference. He would milk the white man; he would ask him for two dollars for the double journey, and he would, quite certainly, get it. The white man had more money than sense. Meanwhile it was pleasant to rest under the sun, its heat mitigated by the strong sea-wind, and bask in the knowledge that no more work need be done for at least a couple of days. Two dollars was a lot of money.

At the sea's edge north-eastern Malaya shed the last tawdry clothes of civilisation. The China Sea yielded fish, the trees coconuts and bananas, the drowned fields a sufficiency of rice. The women wore a single loose garment, the men showed muscular torsos flawed with benignant skin diseases. Idiocy and slow speech were the flower of much endogamy, yaws flourished unchecked by penicillin. Life was short but happy. On the wide sands lay Crabbe and his wife, half-closed eyes taking in a distant diorama of sampans.

Fenella Crabbe displayed firm golden flesh to the huge blue air and Crabbe had never before been so aware of her beauty. But the whole world here breathed easy concupiscence: the bare shoulders of the women, the naked children, the fish-smell, the sea whence life arose, the water that waited, but not passively, to be ravished, the great yellow empty bed of the beach. And so, ardently, he renewed his vows, aware too of his own warm nakedness under the monstrous aphrodisiac of a tropical sun.

"There is such a thing," he said, "as being blind. I acknowledge my blindness with all humility. I shall never be blind again."

"And so you do love me?"

"I do love you. And I want to make amends in any way I can. I want to expiate everything."

"There's a small thing you can do for me."

"Anything."

"I'm going into the water now. I'm going to swim. I want you to come in with me."

Crabbe drew away from her. "You know I can't do that."

"But you said you'd do anything."

"Anything reasonable, anything you need . . ."

"Surely love isn't reasonable, not always? Anyway, this is reasonable, and it's something very small. Come on, Victor, for me. Come and have a swim."

Crabbe turned on her in passion. "Why are you asking me to do this? What's the point of it?"

She sat up and said evenly, "I want to see if you really love me. If you do love me you'll put the past out of your mind. I want you to break with the past. I want there to be only one woman in your life, and that woman to be me. Come on." She rose with grace, long, slim, rounded in the smart meagre bathing-dress. "Come and have a swim."

"I won't. I can't. You know I can't."

"All right, you needn't swim. Just wade in. As far as your armpits. The water's perfectly safe."

Crabbe looked up at her bitterly. She had shrunk to a calendar beauty. The mood of desire and tenderness had gone. "I can't," he repeated. "You know why I can't. If I could overcome that old fear I would. But I don't know how to."

"For years you said you'd never drive a car again. But you do drive a car now. You got over that fear. I want you to get over this."

"I can't."

She smiled, and Crabbe distinctly saw pity in it. "All right. Never mind. I'm going in, anyway."

She ran down the ribs of sand, sending the sand-crabs scurrying to their holes. The sea sent in its flowers of surf along the long coastline, with a tiny rattle of shingle. Fenella strode in, her arms keeping balance as though she walked a tight-rope. The sand shelved gently here. Only at waist-level did the sudden dips occur, and then an upward-sloping hill would lead to a sand-bar, to a new shore islanded in the sea. Fenella strode on, rose to the bar and stood for an instant as if standing on the waves, then entered the new sea-brink, and soon was far out, swimming strongly.

Dejected, Crabbe lay on his stomach, absently tracing capital letters in the sand. Suddenly, with a shock, he saw what name he had been writing. He swiftly passed his fingers over the weak inscription, obliterating it, but not obliterating her. Fenella knew. But she must believe that he was prepared to try, that perhaps in time the past would have no more power over him. After all, no man could give everything. But she wanted him all, wanted every sullen pocket of his memory turned inside out, wanted to fill him with herself, and with herself only. But the past was not part of him; he was part of it. What more could he do? She must accept the Minotaur. The Labyrinth had many rooms, enough for a life together—walls to be covered with shelves and pictures, corridors in which the Beast echoed only once in a score of years.

Fancying he heard Fenella's voice taunting him from the sea he turned over lazily, the sun in his eyes, and saw her far out. He heard her voice again and looked more intently. He thought he saw arms flailing, a churning of the sea around her. He stood up. That voice was certainly calling for help. Heart pounding, he rushed to the sea's edge, straining his eyes narrowly, hoping it was a mistake, a joke. Thinly above the sea-wind her voice called, her body churned the small patch of sea, her arms were wild. He remembered the warnings of treacherous currents, but surely that was only in the monsoon season. Or was it a sea-snake?

Sick with apprehension and hopelessness he walked into the sea. It rose thirstily, higher, lapping round his ankles, shins, knees, thighs, waist. Then, without warning, the shelf plunged a foot or so, and he found himself frantic, feeling the green foam-flowered water round his chest. He panicked, kicked, turned, sobbing, towards the shore. It was no good, it was just no good. He lay panting at the sea's lips, not daring to look back, frantically trying not to hear the thin distant voice.

"All right, darling." Fenella was beside him, comforting him with her wet body. "Perhaps that wasn't fair, really. But I just had to know."

"You're all right?" Relief began to modulate to anger. All that for nothing . . . "You were only pretending?"

"Yes. It's as safe as houses. Safer. Come on, now."

He lay gasping on dry sand, she beside him.

"I just had to know," she repeated, swabbing her face, arms, shoulders, with a towel. "When you thought the bandits had got us you were able to drive the car. You seem able to exorcise demons when you yourself are concerned. It's the old instinct of self-preservation. But if my life only is involved . . ."

"That's not fair. You know it's not fair. Water's elemental, it's an enemy, it's different . . ."

"It's not different. You just couldn't make the effort this time, that's all. It wasn't really important enough. It doesn't matter. I'm not blaming you. But you see now that it won't work. I've known for some time now what I had to do. This was just a rather spectacular way of showing you."

"It wasn't fair. I still say it wasn't fair."

"That doesn't matter. I'm really sorry for you, Victor. I should have had the sense to see before. You've never really been unfaithful to me, because you never started to be faithful. All that stupid business with the Malay girl, and then this affair with Anne Talbot. It didn't mean what it seemed to mean. And now I know what I have to do."

"What have you to do?"

"I have to go home. And perhaps, at leisure, we can arrange a divorce. There isn't any hurry. But it's all been rather a waste of time, hasn't it?"

Crabbe sulked, saying nothing.

"Thank God I'm still young. And you are too. Things will sort themselves out somehow. But not between us. Perhaps I'll find somebody to marry, somebody for whom it will be the first time. And you'll never marry again, I'm quite sure of that. You can go on being faithful to her, which means revelling in guilt. But it isn't fair for anybody to have to feel guilty about two people. You won't have to feel guilty about me again."

He still said nothing.

"And you needn't even feel guilty about the waste of time. It's been a waste of time for both of us equally. And I think perhaps you've suffered the most."

Crabbe said, tonelessly, "What do you want me to do?"

"Get in touch with Federation Establishment. Get them to book me an air passage home. I'm entitled to that. I think you should be able to fix things in about a week."

"And what will you do in England?"

"Oh, there are several things. I shall go back to Maida Vale first of all. Uncle will be glad to see me. And then there are several jobs I can get. The Abang's made me a very tempting offer. He wants me to be a sort of secretary to him. I think I should be good at that. It means travelling around. It will be good to see Europe again. But I haven't decided yet."

"You are cold-blooded, aren't you?"

"Me? Oh, I don't think so. I've just got to make up for lost time, that's all." She pressed his hand, smiling. "Cheer up, darling. It's all for the best, you know."

Crabbe recognised the feeling that passed over his limbs, the pain of life flowing back after cramp, and was surprised to find that it could be called relief.

"Now," she said, "we'd better get back. There's a lot to do, and I can't start too soon."

They trudged back over the sand to the waiting trishaw and woke the snoring driver. In the narrow double seat they sat, as long before, like lovers, his arm round the back of the seat, their bodies crammed together. Paid off in the house drive, the trishaw man gaped in incredulity at the single note. Five dollars! A whole week's holiday. The white man certainly had more money than sense.

17

"But I tell you," said Hardman wearily, "I tell you for the tenth time that she was a client."

'Che Normah walked the length of the sitting-room, did a brisk turn up-stage and resumed her vilifications. It had been reported to her by many, she said, not only Malays, that this Chinese woman had entered his office, dressed shamelessly and provocatively in a high-slit cheongsam, and had stayed closeted with him for an hour. Some said an hour and a half, others an hour and a quarter, yet others an hour and five minutes. But it was certainly an hour. An hour was a long time, much could happen in an hour, one did not spend a whole hour on legal business.

"But it was a complicated business," protested Hardman. "It was about a car accident. It took a long time to get all the details."

She would believe all that when cats had horns. "Ruperet," she said, cooingly, "Ruperet, you must be very, very careful. I expected you to be different from the other two. But you have got drunk and you have been with other women and you have cursed the name of the Prophet in the white man's club."

"I haven't. I haven't looked at another woman." And that was true. Normah was a full-time job. "And I haven't said a word about the Prophet."

"You have said that the Prophet could not read and write."

"But he couldn't. Everybody knows that."

"And the Kathi and the Mufti have been hearing about you and they are saying that you are not a good Moslem. How do you think this makes me appear in the eyes of the town?" Her clear eyes caught the light and flashed silver. "It is me you are making look a fool. But I will not be made to look a fool. The other two discovered that, but they were too late. You I give warning to. There are men up the road who have little axes."

"Oh, I'm sick and tired of hearing about these blasted axes. Haven't the people here anything better to think about than axes, axes, axes?" His voice rose on the repetition—"*Kapak, kapak, kapak.*"

"Ruperet, I will not have you shouting at me. All the time you are shouting."

"I am not shouting," shouted Hardman.

"Because I am kind and forgiving, you try to take advantage all the time."

"Look," said Hardman, getting up from his chair, "I'm going out."

"Oh, no, you are not." She stood, arms folded, by the open door, backed by harsh daylight and coarse greenery. "Your office is closed today. I will not have you going off to see your debauched white friends and skulking behind their closed doors and desecrating the fasting month with drinking. You will stay here with me."

"I have no white friends," he said angrily, "debauched or otherwise. You've seen to that. You got rid of my best friend, you had him thrown out of the State. Just because he was trying to help a dying man. And then you say that Islam is tolerant. Why, Islam is . . ."

"You will not say bad things about religion," she said quietly, undulating a step or two towards him. "I have warned you about that. And that white friend of yours was a very bad man. He was a Christian. He tried to kill that schoolteacher because he had entered the True Faith. He made him eat something bad and he put poison all over his body."

"Oh, you don't know the first thing about it," moaned Hardman. "You just don't want to know, any of you. Look here, I'm going out. Get away from that door."

"I will not. You are not going out."

"I don't want to use force," said Hardman. "But you'd better realise once and for all, that I'm going to have my own way. I'm going to be master. And if you don't get away from that door, I shall . . ."

"What will you do?"

"I'm going out, I tell you. Don't be a fool."

'Che Normah stayed where she was, her magnificent full body confronting his delicate weak white one. Hardman turned, and strode towards the kitchen.

"Now where are you going, Ruperet?"

"I'm going to the *jamban*."

"No, you are not. You think you are going to get out by the back door."

Hardman ran for it. He clattered down the three stone steps to the big cool kitchen, into the yard. But the yard door was locked and the rusty iron key not in its accustomed hole. He heard Normah's light laughter behind him and turned angrily.

"God Almighty, am I supposed to be a prisoner?"

"I have the key and I have also the key of the car."

Hardman leapt lightly on to the dust-bin that stood by

the low yard wall. He scrambled on to the top of the wall and prepared to jump.

"Ruperet! I will not have you making a fool of me! Come back at once!"

Hardman jumped into the street, surveyed by two open-mouthed Malay workmen with dish-towels round their heads.

"Mad," one said to the other.

"They are all mad."

"Ruperet!"

Hardman ran to the corner and jumped into a trishaw. The driver was maddeningly slow and stupid.

"*Mana, tuan?*"

"Anywhere. No, wait. To the Haji Ali College. To the house of the *guru besar.*"

"I do not know where that is, *tuan.*"

"Get going, quick!" urged Hardman. "Round this corner."

Many men, women and children, clothed in bright raiment for the Sabbath, saw with a faint flicker of interest and surprise a very white man on a trishaw, and the driver pedalling with unseemly haste. Allah, his creditors were after him, or an axe-man, or perhaps his wife. The patterns of the East are few.

'So it has come to this,' thought Hardman, as they sped down the main road. 'My only refuge is a man who believes I have wronged him. But he will help, he must help.' He looked behind him once more, but there was still no sign of the pursuing Fury. He took a deep breath and drew from the breast pocket of his wet shirt a letter which he had received at the office the previous day, a letter already much crumpled, read and re-read.

My dear Hardman,

It was pleasant to hear from you after all these years. I am sorry that your Oriental venture has not been going as well as you expected. But, then, I think that the days when a man could expect to make his fortune in the East are dead and gone. Indeed, the time seems to have come for the reverse of the old process to apply, and for the East to dominate the West. We have here, in at least two Departments, very able lecturers with unpronounceable Indian names, and they are the life and soul of Faculty meetings. There seems to be a certain energy there which has long burnt itself out in Europe. However, this is as may be. I was interested in your inquiry about the possibility of your joining the Department. It so happens that there is a vacancy for a Junior Lecturer, occasioned by Gilkes being appointed (you will remember Gilkes?) to the Law Faculty of a rather disreputable minor university in, I think, Louisiana, or certainly one of the southern states of America. He wrote a book, you may remember, on the Napoleonic Code, and now he will have an opportunity to devote his life to reproducing it to young men with crew-cuts. The book was, I thought, ill-written. However, this post falls vacant in October. The salary of a Junior Lecturer is, as you know, not high, and you may find it hard to adjust yourself to a life without the luxuries which the East has, undoubtedly, accustomed you to taking for granted. However, do write and let me know if you would definitely like to be considered for this post and I will set the machinery in motion.

With all good wishes,

Yours sincerely,
E. F. Goodall.

And now he must raise the fare. He remembered that Crabbe had told him about his getting a share of a lottery prize in Kuala Hantu. Surely a loan of, say, two thousand dollars was not out of the way? After all, they were united by the tenuous cord of blood and a common Alma Mater.

Hardman saw himself, heart beating with hope and excitement, catching the plane from Singapore, watching that island drop down out of his life, and, behind it, the slim limb of the peninsula which he never wanted to see again. About leaving Normah he had no qualms. She could keep the car and his law books and the small balance in the bank. After all, she was entitled to that—restitution of the *mas kahwin* on the husband's desertion. And, once he was back in England, she could have no further claim on him, outside the tentacles of Islamic law, for the marriage had no secular legal status.

And there he would be, back in the pleasant musty smell of the Law Faculty, with Professor Goodall and his nicotined moustache, his pipe that would not draw, and there would be arguments about torts and statutes, and the soothing droning voices of the world where he really belonged, the rain and the weekly papers, the clanking trams and the sooty trees and the girl students in jumpers and silk stockings. But no, it was all nylon now. The world changed behind one's back.

Behind his back there was only the dusty road and a vista of barren coconut palms. He reached the cluster of Malay houses that enclosed Crabbe, paid off the driver, and, his throat dry, climbed the steps that led to Crabbe's veranda. The house was silent and, he thought, rather dusty. There were patches on the walls where pictures had been and no flowers in the vases. Hardman stealthily walked into the open sitting-room. There was no carpet on the floor, only the ghost of the carpet defined in an oblong of unpolished wood. The desk looked alive, however, littered as it was with papers and files and letters. Hardman could not help seeing one letter, clumsily typed:

H.H. The Abang,
The Istana,
Kenching.

This is to inform Your Highness that I have instructed Messrs. Tan Cheong Po, Motor-Car Agents and Garage, Kenching, to deliver my Abelard car to the Istana, so that it may form part of Your Highness's collection. I am afraid that the car is not in first-class condition and I hope Your Highness will pardon this. However, it is perhaps appropriate that one of the last of the Western expatriates should bequeath to an Oriental potentate all that the West seems now to be able to offer to the East, namely, a burnt-out machine.

Your Highness's to Command,
Victor Crabbe.

Hardman walked quietly down the dusty corridor and peered over the half-doors of the main bedroom. There, at high noon, Crabbe lay in bed, unshaven, hair too long, smoking and reading Toynbee. Crabbe looked up blearily. On the bedside table were a bottle of gin, a jug of water, and a glass.

"Who is it? What the hell are you doing here?"

"A friendly visit. And an apology, if you'll take it." Hardman came into the room. A toad hopped out of his way.

"Come in. Sit down on the other bed. Pour yourself a drink."

Hardman sat on the cold unused twin bed. "Have you heard from your wife?" he asked.

"A letter yesterday."

"I'm sorry about that business, Victor. It was sheer carelessness on my part. I ask you to believe there was nothing malicious in it."

"That? Oh, that doesn't matter any more. See, she sent me quite a long letter. I'd forgotten how well she can write." Crabbe took up thin blue sheets from the floor beside his bed. "She said it was quite a good trip. Everything was a bit of a shambles at Karachi, but Beirut, she says, is a fine place. They stop off at Beirut now, since the Cyprus trouble."

"Trouble everywhere."

"Yes. Do you remember a chap called Raffles?"

Was Crabbe going off his head? Was history becoming a timeless dream for him? "You don't mean Stamford?"

"No, it's definitely Raffles. A rather nice little Jew at the Technical College."

"Oh, *that* Raffles."

"Yes. Fenella met him at Beirut airport. Apparently he's running a small air service of his own now. A couple of Beavers, and he's going to get another. He does a trip from Jiddah up to the Lebanon and now he's extending it as far as Marseilles."

"Where's Jiddah?"

"Oh, that's near Mecca. You should know, being a good Muslim. That's the port that serves the cradle of your faith."

"Victor, I want to go home."

"But you've only just come," said Crabbe, pouring

out gin for himself, handing the bottle to Hardman.

"No, *real* home. I've been offered a job at the university. Lecturer in the Law Faculty."

"Well, congratulations. But I thought things were going all right here, from the financial point of view, I mean. I thought you were settling down."

"I've got to get away," said Hardman with passion. "She's killing me."

"Really?" Crabbe rested on his elbow, looking at Hardman with bleary interest. "You mean, that's what she's trying to do? I must say you're not looking at all well. You've lost weight. Are they making wax images of you and burning them over a slow fire? I'm sure that's what's happening with me. I feel lousy."

"Is that why you stay in bed?"

"Oh, there's just nothing to get up for."

"Look here, Victor," plunged Hardman, "can you lend me two thousand dollars? I can pay you back when I get home. I can send you monthly instalments."

"Two thousand? That's a lot of money. Have you tried any of these money-lenders in the town?"

"I daren't," said Hardman. "Everybody would know about it. *She'd* know."

"It's a lot of money."

"You could do it, Victor. You're the only man I can come to. You're the only one I can trust."

Crabbe lay on his bed, hands folded as in death, and gazed at the cobwebbed ceiling. "You don't trust me all that much. Any more than I trust you."

"Oh, that's all over. But, don't you see, I've got to raise the fare home. You've got the money, I know you have. You told me."

"Did I?"

"Yes. You got part of a lottery prize. You told me. That friend of yours won the first prize and he gave you a cut."

"Nabby Adams. Yes. And now he's in Bombay. We're all leaving. We're all deserting Malaya. It doesn't want us any more."

"Come on, Victor, for old times' sake. Your money will be as safe as houses. You'll get it back. With interest, if you like."

"I haven't got it. I gave it to Fenella. It was hers as much as it was mine."

"All of it?" asked Hardman.

"All of it. I don't need much money." Crabbe continued to lie, eyes slowly following the questing flight of a mason-wasp, flat on his back, hands folded.

"Well," sulked Hardman, "if you won't help . . ."

"I can't help, old boy. I wish I could. I just can't, that's all. Do have some more gin."

"I haven't had any. I don't see how I can very well have more."

"Yes. Like *Alice*. Alice, where art thou?" Crabbe lay on his side, his face turned away from Hardman.

"Are you tight, Victor?"

"Not tight. Just lousy. Just not very well. Do come and see me again. Call any time. Always glad to see an old friend." His voice faded out on the last two words.

At two in the afternoon, the house silent again, the spiders busy, a toad still flopping about the room, the mason-wasp still seeking a suitable building site, Crabbe lay awake, thinking: 'Am I really such a swine? The insurance money's there, doing . nothing. It would have been a friendly act.'

He raised himself up stiffly, looking for a cigarette, and thought: 'He's made his bed; he's got to lie on it. Which

reminds me that this bed needs making. I'd better get up.'
But he lay there still, hearing the clock march jauntily on
to three o'clock, four o'clock, having nothing to get up for.

At nightfall Hardman returned, righteously indignant.
He had spent part of the afternoon in the Field Force mess,
hidden from the sharp eyes of Islam, drinking gloomy
beer. There he had met Inche Mat bin Anjing, also hiding
from the sharp eyes of Islam, drinking beer not so gloomy.
Inche Mat was a local insurance agent. He informed Hardman that Crabbe had a cheque for two thousand dollars
waiting for him in the office, this being the amount for
which Crabbe's car had been insured, and that Crabbe had
not yet troubled to come and collect it.

Hardman stumbled into the dark house, switching on
lights, surprising *chichaks* scurrying over the walls. He
went down to Crabbe's bedroom and assaulted his eyes
with a harsh flood of light, showing up tossed bedclothes,
scattered books and papers, hopping toads, Crabbe wide
awake, his beard darker, his hair wilder.

"What the hell?"

"Aren't you ever going to get up? Come on, out of it."

"I'll stay in bed if I want to."

"You lied to me."

"What do you mean, lied?"

"You've got two thousand dollars. I know. Insurance
money on your car. I was told this afternoon."

"What's that got to do with you?"

"Lend it me. Damn it all, you said you would if you
could."

"And so you whizz around in your big Jaguar, lord of
the earth, and I'm expected to go about on foot, is that it?
Damn it, man, I've got to buy a new car."

"You could hire a car, you could use trishaws. In any

case, you don't seem so very anxious to do any getting about. In bed all day."

"That's my business."

Hardman sat on the bed, saying, "I daren't go home."

"That's all right, then. You don't need two thousand dollars."

"No, no. I daren't go back to her, to her house."

" 'Home' is an equivocal term. Fenella was always saying that. Spend the night here if you like."

"Have you eaten anything?"

"No."

But soon Talbot came, making sure that no man should starve. Into the bedroom he brought the meagre stocks of the store-cupboard—tinned cheese, sardines, cocktail sausages, Brand's Chicken Essence, a ragged loaf, a basin of dripping, a cold leg of lamb, H.P. sauce and the salt-cellar.

"What's happened to your cook?" asked Talbot, munching, spilling crumbs on the bed.

"I don't need a cook any more."

"And your amah?"

"She's a lazy little bitch."

Later that evening Police Constable Kartar Singh came, accompanied by two Sikh friends. Crabbe protested that he didn't need police protection any more, that there was nothing to protect any more. Kartar Singh said that, if he did not mind, he would continue to protect the sahib, helped now by his friend Teja Singh who had lost his job as night-watchman and might as well sleep here as anywhere else. This was, if the sahib did not mind him saying so, a cushy billet, and he would be obliged if the sahib would say nothing to the Officer Commanding Police District about no longer requiring police protection.

Mohinder Singh sat gloomy, seeing in vision his life-blood dripping away as the shop's trade worsened, as the Bengalis and Tamils and Chinese counted fat takings and no man came to the shop of Mohinder Singh.

So, round the bed of Victor Crabbe, beer was drunk and cheese eaten, and more beer was sent out for. Finally Hardman lay down on the other bed, saying to Crabbe:

"Think about it, Victor. Think how much it means to me. I'll pay you back, every cent of it."

Crabbe pretended to be asleep.

18

They were roasting him over a slow fire, a human barbecue. Jaganathan supervised the turning and the basting, saying often: "They are good peoples. You are good peoples and I am good peoples. We are all good peoples." Talbot dripped fat over his spitted carcase, expressing worry, finally bringing in a doctor who smelled deliciously of spirits and talked of pyrexia of unknown origin. The word 'pyrexia' began to turn and topple like a snowball going downhill, smashing itself on a black winter tree to reveal a core of stone which meant 'fire'. It also meant her putting the casserole in the oven to cook slowly while they went to hear the violinist playing the César Franck sonata. She talked animatedly about the canon in the last movement, the cyclical form, deploring the romantic treacle which glued up the neo-classicism. Talbot showed interest in the treacle and recited a passage from *Piers Plowman* about the treacle of heaven. He ate this with a spoon, waiting till the Pyrex dish be drawn from the oven. In the dish was a baked crab.

The cannon in the last movement boomed the end of the fasting month, because one spied the little crescent all were seeking. Jaganathan came to weep tears of basting fat and to say that the fight was on. There was a list of names of angry parents who had signed the petition that had not yet been written, an anthology of Oriental scripts. The amah, frightened, came in to sweep the room. Toads hopped in front of her.

When Crabbe felt cooler he heard the voice of Abdul Kadir saying, "For fuck's sake, take your finger out. That was a bloody good article about the revolution in the East. It's the truth, and I told him it's the truth. People starving and not enough rice to go round. Unfortunately they know all about you in Kuala Lumpur, going to a hotel with another man's wife. Otherwise they'd let you bring in the revolution."

Revolution of a cycle of Cathay. Where was Hardman? Hardman never came.

The fire returned, the eternal basting, the sheet soaked in hot fat. The man who smelled of whisky talked about hospitals. Talbot said leave it till tomorrow.

In the hot night the light was switched on. Crabbe heard the voice of an old man, happily chirping. The old man was giving him something to drink, something red-hot. Crabbe lay exhausted. The room was full of people, but this was no surprise; for a long time now the room had been full of people, some dead, some alive, some here, some eight thousand miles away. Crabbe tried to focus. One man spoke good English with a Chinese high school accent.

"I don't quite understand," said Crabbe.

"It is the amnesty. It was in the newspaper wrapped round the rice. The Government will ask no more questions. They will pay fares to China."

"I will pay his fare to England," said Crabbe. "I always meant to. But I couldn't get up. And he's not been round to see me. Look here, you're all Chinese."

"We are all Chinese. We want to go back to China. So Ah Wing brings us to you."

"But I can't raise all that much money. I can only find enough for the fare to England. And only for him."

"Perhaps you are ill. I cannot quite understand what you're saying."

"Wait," said Crabbe. He tried to sit up. Ah Wing came round to support him. "Just give me a minute. What's going on, anyway?"

"We have come out of the jungle. It was no good staying there. It was difficult to get food. You helped us for a long time. Then you could not help us any more. But we thank you for the help you gave us while you could."

"No, no," said Crabbe. He saw the young man more clearly. "I didn't give any help. I wouldn't. You're a lot of . . . A lot of . . ."

"So now we come to give ourselves up. You have a telephone here. But they must keep their promise."

"Who?"

"The police. The Government. They must not play tricks on us."

Whatever Ah Wing had given him had induced clarity, even a sort of drunken cotton-wool euphoria. Crabbe looked round the room at some ten or twelve Chinese, some in ragged uniform, some in old shirts and faded grey trousers. One or two had rifles.

"That's a woman," said Crabbe.

"Yes, that is Rose. And I am Boo Eng. Ah Wing is the father of my wife. My wife died under the Japanese."

"What do you want me to do?" asked Crabbe.

"You can telephone the police and say that we give ourselves up if the Government will play fair."

"Play fair?" said Crabbe. "Where did you learn that expression?"

"I used to play basketball at school."

"Surely," said Crabbe, "there's a policeman round here somewhere. I seem to remember that there was a police guard round the house or something. I've been ill, you see. It was all Jaganathan's fault. He was sticking pins in me. Or burning me. I am not sure which."

"There is a fat Sikh outside the house. He is asleep. He has a friend who is also asleep."

Crabbe tried to get up. He felt very weak. He was supported by Ah Wing and a grim young man with long black hair. It seemed somehow wrong for a Chinese to have long hair.

"Take your time, Mr. Crabbe. There is no great hurry."

Crabbe was assisted down the corridor to the sitting-room. Dust lay everywhere, and on a table was a pile of newspapers, delivered punctually but unread, a calendar of his illness. "What a mess," he said. Then, "Who do I ask for?"

"This is a matter for the C.P.O. It is a big matter."

Crabbe heard voices from the kitchen. "Are there others in there?" he said.

"Oh, yes. There are perhaps thirty of us. You will not mind if some of them have a little food. Ah Wing has boiled rice for them and we found some tins of meat in your store-room."

Shakily Crabbe made for the telephone. "Look here," he said. "What time is it? I've just no idea."

Boo Eng consulted a Rolex wrist-watch. "It is now one o'clock in the morning. You had best contact the C.P.O. at his house. There will only be fools at the police station now."

Obediently Crabbe asked for the C.P.O.'s house. His voice sounded drunk and the C.P.O., sleepy and annoyed, was inclined to slam the telephone down. But when Crabbe mentioned the name Boo Eng the C.P.O.'s voice became alert, as though it had put on a uniform.

"Boo Eng, you say?"

"That's the name."

"Good God, man, hang on. Don't do a thing. Keep them there. Have you got a gun?"

"Not at the moment. But I think I can get one."

Obligingly one of the Communist terrorists handed to Crabbe a small automatic pistol. It contained no ammunition. Obligingly another woke up Kartar Singh and his companion. It seemed only fair to let them share in the glory.

"You know," said Crabbe, "that stuff of Ah Wing's is pretty good. I feel a good deal better. Weak, of course, but that's inevitable. I wonder if Ah Wing would be good enough to make some tea?"

"He is still your servant. You did not give him notice, he did not give you notice. Of course he will make you tea."

"And what was in that medicine?"

"It is very powerful. It is tiger's liver stewed in brandy. It is better than all the European medicines."

Crabbe made the headlines. And, when the headlines were forgotten, the story still ran around the *kampongs*, of how the white man, though dying of fever, had captured single-handed thirty dangerous Communist terrorists. As, convalescing, he sat on his veranda in the cool dusk, the Malays began to gather round him once more, forgetting the time when they had their doubts about him, the stories they had languidly listened to about his being the enemy of mankind.

Crabbe told them his story, much-embroidered, for pure truth is not relished in the East. Some day, he knew, the tale would pass into timeless legend, and Crabbe's heroic feat would become one of the exploits of Hang Tuah, the brave Laksamana of Malacca, or, in lighter vein, be transmuted to a cunning trick played by the fabulous Mousedeer on a whole herd of elephants.

When Crabbe returned to his sweltering office in Haji Ali College, Jaganathan looked up from the loaded important desk with surprise and pleasure.

"Mr. Crabbe, I knew all the time that you were good peoples."

"Thank you, Mr. Jaganathan." Jaganathan did not get up. Crabbe, weak still, took a chair from one of the Malay clerks.

"You should have told me earlier that you had applied for transfer, Mr. Crabbe. I cannot understand that you did not say before. It would have saved so much trouble for both of us."

"A transfer, Mr. Jaganathan?"

"Yes. You are to be moved. Perhaps you have not yet heard?"

"No, I haven't."

"I hear these things often before other people. It is a question of knowing clerks in the right places, that is all. It is always the clerks who know."

Jaganathan was right. Crabbe went to see Talbot almost at once, taking the long painful road to the town in a trishaw. He had not yet bought another second-hand car. The insurance cheque for two thousand dollars still lay snug in the office of Inche Mat bin Anjing. In the Education Office Talbot was enjoying his elevenses—a dish of smoking *mee*, a couple of curry puffs, a glass of murky iced coffee.

"Come in, Victor. You might as well get to know your

new place of work. I'm sorry I've not been able to tell you the glad news before now. There's been such a hell of a lot to do. You're taking my place. You're going to be C.E.O."

"Let's have that again, slowly. I'm still weak, remember."

"You're taking over. I'm going to K.L. I don't suppose you'll be more than a temporary fill-in until they've found a Malay to take your place. This State's being Malayanised pretty fast, and all the top jobs are going to Malays. The Indians and Chinese aren't going to like it, but there it is. This is a Malay State. I suppose you'll be following me fairly soon, into the citadel. All the Europeans will be drawing into the centre. The end is nigh."

"The night in which no man can work."

"I wouldn't say that, you know. Nothing's permanent, there's always enough time if you make enough time. I'd say we've got to work now as we've never worked before. But not in the classroom and not in the office. We've just got to talk to people, that's all. Talk to them over a meal, over a couple of whiskies, try and give them a bit of a friendly warning, a bit of advice. Try and get them to think a bit. We didn't need to do that in the old days. We did the thinking for them. Now we've really got to teach them. Rapidly, earnestly, under pressure. I've written a poem about that. I've got it here somewhere." He rummaged in a crammed in-tray. "This is only a first draft. It needs tidying up, but I think you'll get the general idea." In his harsh flat voice, without nuances, he intoned his lines. The clerks took no notice, being used to him.

"In moments of crisis hunger comes, welling
    Up through the groaning tubes, and feeding-time

Is the time of waking or perhaps the time before
Night settles on the land, endless night.
Light, whether of dawn or evening, turns
The river to glow-gold syrup, the trees
To a fairyland of fruit. . . ."

His mouth watering slightly, Talbot put down the manuscript. "You get the general idea," he said.

"Who's going to be Head of Haji Ali College?" asked Crabbe.

"Oh, yes, One in the eye for old Jaganathan. They want a Malay, you see, and the one with most service is Abdul Kadir. I daresay Kadir will be all right. Perhaps this promotion will sober him up a bit."

"Well," said Crabbe. "For fuck's sake."

After leaving Talbot's office Crabbe collected his two thousand dollars from Inche Mat bin Anjing. Then he sought Hardman. But Hardman's business premises were locked up, and none of the towkays in the shops on either side had any information. And the house also was empty. Noobdy seemed to know anything of the whereabouts of either Hardman or 'Che Normah.

Except Haji Zainal Abidin. In the early afternoon Crabbe visited him. His house was a two-roomed wooden structure on high stilts, a rickety wooden stair leading from the yard—loud with chickens and children—to the dark warm hole of the living-room. In this living-room sat Haji Zainal Abidin's wife, busy at a Japanese sewing-machine, surrounded by further children. She was a handsome black-browed woman, her nose hooked and Arab. In Malay she told Crabbe that her husband was asleep, that she dare not wake him. She also gave Crabbe a frank come-hither glance which Crabbe ignored.

In Haji Zainal Abidin's sleeping brain the purdah curtain twitched, his wife showed her face to the intruder. Haji Zainal Abidin awoke and came into the living-room, clad in a striped sarong and a pyjama jacket, the best of both worlds.

"My dear fellow," he said. "I am honoured. What have we? Have we whisky? Brandy? There is only Wincarnis which my wife takes for her anæmia. Where is our Number One son? At school. Our Number Two? Only Number Five, and he cannot be trusted. It is a fat lot of use having children when they cannot be trusted to carry out even the simplest mission. Very well, we shall send little Hadijah to the corner shop. She shall bring us some beer."

"You're very kind," said Crabbe, "but I didn't really intend to stay."

"And so," said Haji Zainal Abidin, "because I am only a Malay you will not accept my hospitality. Because I am only a poor bloody Malay and do not live in a fine European house with a fan spinning all the time. I tell you, you English bastard, there will never be peace on earth until the Europeans have learned to treat their black brothers like brothers. Intolerance all the time." He offered Crabbe a cigarette and noisily ordered a small pretty child to find matches.

"I'm looking for Hardman," said Crabbe. "Nobody seems to know where he is."

"Hardman," said Haji Zainal Abidin, "my son in God. Hardman has gone away for a time. He has gone on the pilgrimage. He has seen the light."

"Do you mean he's gone to Mecca?"

"Where else would he go on the pilgrimage? I tell you, ignorance will kill the hopes of the world."

"Has he gone alone?"

Haji Zainal Abidin laughed loudly, showing his uncountable teeth and his red gullet. "He wished to go alone, but his wife would not let him. She said she had as much right as he to become a *haji* and, besides, it is her money. What she says is true, but it is a pity for Hardman. The Arab women are the loveliest in the world, the only ones for which a man could have any appetite. Any *appetite*." With appetite he stared at his wife who simpered coyly at Crabbe. "So you see," said Haji Zainal Abidin, "Hardman will come back a *haji*. Like me, a *haji*. But a very junior *haji*. I am the senior *haji* round here. I am—" he paused before delivering the *mot juste*—"the prototypical *haji*. Do you know that word? Prototypical. I say that word to my boss this morning and he does not know the meaning. To think that I speak the white man's tongue better than the white man." He laughed harshly and long, but still with appetite in his eyes. Crabbe judged that it was now time to leave. Haji Hardman. Well . . .

19

I have to talk to somebody or to something. I will talk to paper, a thing I have not done since I was at school. This is the diary of a Pilgrim's Progress. She, sleeping in the narrow bunk, thinks that our terminus is Mecca. She is wrong as far as I am concerned. I am going home. Raffles remembered me—but, indeed, who that has ever known me could forget this face that I see now, looking up for a moment, in the mirror of the dressing-table? The face of a very white man, one whom the sun would not accept. Though those scars are new, stigmata that Raffles has not seen. I'll say there is much kindness in the Jew. He knew of my flying career. He says that he will lend me a plane if I will take a small cargo home with me. I do not propose to inquire into the nature of the cargo. He says that the man who is on leave will bring back the plane. It seems a very sensible arrangement.

She turns over in her sleep and utters a single harsh Malay word that I do not know, that I do not wish to know. The Indian Ocean glints through the port-hole and the whole rumbling ship is asleep in the Indian Ocean afternoon. A pilgrim ship. Not like the pilgrim ships of *Lord Jim,* a mass of arms and legs and snoring mouths, page after page of them, a squalid net full of fish and broken crab-legs and tentacles, heaving in sleep towards Mecca.

Crabbe might have helped. He could have helped. Only when I am on solid English ground, under rain and northern winds, clad in my gown again, back to the world I should never have left, only then will I think of forgiving him. And what do I do about the Church? We'll see about that. Georges wasn't exactly a shining witness, ready to sell his soul to be back in China. Poor Georges. And who is saying about me: 'Poor Rupert?' Stop feeling bloody sorry for yourself.

There are people here who cook their food on the decks. There are others who have rice thrown to them, like chickens. They gobble up the rice with a sea-air appetite. Our food is not too bad. Curries mostly. It will be good to be free of the eternal rice, away from the rice-myths, back to the corn-myths, bread and wine.

Normah isn't eating much. She's been seasick a good deal. I can always feel sorry for people who are being sick. And when I can feel pity for her that's easily turned into a sort of love. What made her like that, I wonder? She's not hungry for me or for any man. Perhaps if she'd had a child it would have been different. And now it's too late. In the East women want to identify themselves with their biological function. And that makes them all woman. Compartmentalisation is our big crime in the West. Normah should have been the Great Earth Mother. Frustration in her tears at the world with ravening claws, the world being man. It will soon be time for tea.

June 16th.

The ship is a Dutch ship. I seem to be the only white pilgrim, and most of the Asiatic passengers seem to take me for a member of the crew, perpetually off duty. One

Indonesian this morning addressed me in Dutch. Normah, from her languid deck-chair, answered for me. This led to a fascinating monologue about her first husband, Willem, and how she did for him after all his wickedness, drunkenness, perfidy. She has great hopes for me now and says frankly that she doubts if she will ever have to call the axe-men in. It is enough that I have realised my wickedness and repented. God will forgive the repentant sinner. She sees the two of us entering heaven, hand in hand, both clad in the shining costume of pilgrims. She then suggested that we repair to our cabin for a while but I said I did not feel very well.

True enough. I played cards and drank secret gin with the chief engineer, the ship's doctor and the restaurateur in the chief's cabin last night. Normah believed that I had gone to a reading of the Koran.

June 17th.

Colombo and a few more pilgrims. Normah did not feel like leaving her bunk. I thought, with a sort of luxurious sensuality, as the launch took a number of sightseeing passengers to the misty island through moist northern-seeming sea-air, that now I could, if I wanted, make the break. But I wouldn't get very far. And undoubtedly she would suddenly turn up to drag me back by the ear, creating one of her all too special scenes, magnificent and all too much war. At Jiddah I must be very careful.

Most of the books in the ship's library are in Dutch. And so, strangely enough, and to Normah's great pleasure, I have been reading an English translation of the Koran. I wonder how, with such a repetitive farrago of platitudes, expressing so self-evident a theology and an ethic so puerile, Islam can have spread as it has. And then I remember that

I am, officially, a Muslim. Nay, I am even a Muslim pilgrim.

This afternoon mail comes aboard. There is a letter for me. Raffles is really a good chap. He says it will be a midnight matter and how to get from Mecca to Jiddah late at night and where to meet him or the Arab who works for him. He knows a man who will do the sixty or so miles for me fairly cheaply. He is, strangely enough, a Malay pilgrim who decided to stay in Mecca, who makes money enough with a coughing taxi from the Holy City to the port.

June 18th.
Normah sick again this morning, despite calm sea. I write this drunk, having had bottle of Bols with the Second Officer in his naughty cabin plastered with brassière advertisements. This I say not right for pilgrim ship. I tell him that good Muslim not tolerate such pornography in holy boat. He say to hell and more Bols, Bols being the operative word. He say has girl in Hull, admire English though such bloody fools. Out like light afternoon on bottom bunk, she sleep on top bunk. Haha.

June 20.
Granted that the whole problem of life is integration, who is to tell us how to integrate and what do we mean when we say a man is thoroughly integrated? If we mean man is balanced and knows what he wants, I say he is a pipe-smoking moron with the sort of laugh that I associate only with stupidity or madness. For I would say that it is death to be properly integrated, for then there is no change and one is independent of change in the world about one. I would be as I am, a thin and white nervous wreck, having

made a marriage that becomes more and more fantastic as we travel towards Aden, demi-paradise, and, having, in prospect, an Arabian Nights tale to tell to the cosy Western world reading its evening paper on the Underground. Hurray. The doctor is a very good man and he has cherry brandy in his cabin and tonight he reads to me from Robert Herrick, whose work he likes. Now why should he like Robert Herrick? I mean, what is there in that lustful lyrical Devonshire parson to appeal to a fat stolid medical man from Hilversum? And they talk about integration! Pah!

June 23rd.

Coming to Aden through dolphin-jubilant Arabian Sea. Normah has been to see doctor. He says what she will not believe. I do not believe it either. He says no possible doubt. Discuss this with doctor and second officer over Bols, followed by cherry brandy.

Ah, the shimmer of sea over the taffrail! The phosphorescent night, illuminating in marine benediction what one gives to the deep. Man is never so much alone, never so completely to grips with the fundamental problem of integration as when, under the mast and the steady star, he yields to the sea what the sea will but too readily take. And, flopping on the bench on C Deck, the lines by Blake sing out:

> Him Moira found dwelling in highest bliss,
> Creating gods (no ecstasy like this.)
> Took him, as, calmed by flowers of Beulah, Los,
> Or conscious Christ on an adventitious cross.

Moira being Fate, which the Orientals render Kismet.

June 24th.

Broiling in the Red Sea. It is the humidity. I gasp for air over a game of chess with the Chief Engineer, choking, throwing away twice-puffed cigarettes. I had forgotten it was like this. Shirts stick transparent to men's backs, women go slowly by on the deck, each exhibiting, through a dress like soaked paper, the straps of a brassière. And so we approach the Holy City.

June 25th.

Normah is definitely pregnant. She lies in her bunk, transformed, transfigured. I may go off to do what I like. I flirted with the Dutch stewardess who, a large blonde from Ryswyck, breathed Edam cheese after her kisses. I decide that the East has definitely spoiled me for women. Sitting with the doctor late at night, I see with shock through Herrick and cherry brandy that I have left something of myself in the East. That omphalic cord will pull like rubber over eight thousand miles. I can never be the same again.

June 27th.

We approach the port, Normah's fingers clasped in mine. For the first time in their lives the pilgrims bend towards the East. They have come home. I have come home, or nearly. Gods of the soaring wing and steady engine, fail me not. My big day is coming. I too bend towards the East.

20

"But we must put this on a commercial basis. That is only fair."

All day long the cars had passed, a gleaming butter-smooth convoy, towards the port. The Abang was going. The lights were going on on Jalan Laksamana, two dark gaps in the row of shops like gold-filled teeth.

"Brother, I have done so much for you in the past. I have been your financial prop and stay. Come now, this is but a small return for many kindnesses. Moreover, it is a thing I cannot take seriously."

"Not take seriously? But it is a science, it is based on a philosophy of the universe, it requires considerable train-ing and skill."

Teja Singh set up his bed outside the Grand Hotel, ready to guard the residents, the casual eaters and drinkers, the fat woman who was in charge and the thin dark woman who entertained the business men from Penang and Bangkok. Teja Singh yawned as he sat down, admiring the schoolmaster's new second-hand car.

Kartar Singh, two shining stripes on his sleeve, smiled full-beardedly at his co-religionist who bent his turban over the fat uncomplicated palm, examining the exiguous head-line, the thick line of luck, the plump hump of Venus.

Victor Crabbe smiled faintly from his high stool by the bar. Next to him was perched Abdul Kadir, blinking above tie and clean shirt and creased trousers, sipping a small beer.

"I still cannot understand," said Abdul Kadir. "It is not as if I were a really good man. Not like our Mr. Din, for instance, who has an Indian degree and does not drink and does not swear very much."

"Grace falleth where it will," said Crabbe. "There is nothing that anybody can do about it."

"It is a very strange world," said Abdul Kadir.

Crabbe scrutinised again the photograph on the front page of the *Singapore Bugle*. It showed Chinese terrorists boarding the ship that would take them to their Mecca, to the land of hard work and drab grey uniform for all and sufficient rations and not much fun, his own undergraduate Utopia. Forget about that, forget about her blue jumper and her records of Shostakovitch, her warm white neck and the solace of her compact and willing body while the casserole simmered in the oven of their flat, the woman he could not leave alone. And that particular face, smiling wryly above the squat Chinese bodies, the large mouth and the frank eyes, the crew-cut, surely he knew that face?

"And how do you find the house?" asked Crabbe.

"It is a bloody good house. I mean," said Abdul Kadir, "I like the house very much. But it is too good for the likes of me."

"You learnt that humility from the lower deck," said Crabbe. "Come on, enter into your inheritance, remember that this is your country."

"But it does not seem right," said Abdul Kadir. "It is something new, a white man giving up his house for me, and himself living in a little hotel room. I cannot understand it."

"The house is tied to the College," said Crabbe. "It is

the headmaster's house. Moreover, the Englishman has but a small family or else no family at all. Or even," he added, "no wife. Don't worry about me. In the West we're shrivelling up. We're dried fruit. And we're used to far less luxury than you think."

"Have a fucking beer," said Abdul Kadir. His owlish eyes showed sudden shock. "I mean, have a beer, Mr. Crabbe."

Two Malay workmen entered, dish-towels fastened, turban-wise, about their heads. They ordered orange crush.

"Still here," said one. "The white sods are still here."

"And those turbaned prawns with shit in their heads. But it won't be long now."

"No, it won't be long."

"And that Malay woman is going to have a baby. She is *bunting*."

"*Hamil* is a politer word."

"Why use a polite word? It is the child of that white sod who has gone."

"He has gone for ever."

"What does the bloody postman know? His bundles of letters from England. And the telegrams from England. He is hiding, hiding from everybody, from women in England as well as here."

"They say he was burned."

"That was before, in the second world *perang*."

"His flying ship fell in a cold country. Else why should the Malay woman cry? What will happen to a man once will happen again."

"Good riddance to the sod."

Crabbe remembered his final story to the Malays on the veranda. The story of the man from the far country who tried to help, the man who developed miraculous powers, killing the pirates and the bandits and diseases and teaching the final marvel of the word. And as he developed wings and an unconquerable fist and the gift of invulnerability he ceased to be a man from a far country, he joined the heroes of the Malay Valhalla, he became the property of the open-mouthed tough brown men, cross-legged on the veranda, he became one of them. And Crabbe's final *pantun* as his goods were loaded on to the truck:

> *Kalau tuan mudek ka-hulu,*
> *Charikan saya bunga kemoja.*
> *Kalau tuan mati dahulu,*
> *Nantikan saya di-pintu shurga.*

"Translate it for me, Kadir. Translate it for all the world."

"If you go up the river," translated Kadir, the glaze of drink in his eyes, "pluck me, pluck me . . . For fuck's sake, I've forgotten the word."

"Frangipani."

"Frangipani. But if you die first, wait for me . . ."

"At the door of heaven."

"At the door of heaven. For fuck's sake, man, what are you crying for? Have another fucking beer."

"Your language, Kadir."

"You have very lucky face, Mr. Crabbe," said Mohinder Singh. "You have face of a very lucky gentleman. If you will sit down here for a moment, for two dollars only I will foretell lucky future."

THE UNIFORM EDITION OF
ANTHONY BURGESS

THE MALAYAN TRILOGY
Time for a Tiger
The Enemy in the Blanket
Beds in the East

Devil of a State
The Doctor is Sick
The Right to an Answer
The Worm and the Ring

ALSO BY ANTHONY BURGESS

A Clockwork Orange
Enderby Outside
Inside Mr Enderby
(*as Joseph Kell*)
One Hand Clapping
(*as Joseph Kell, published by Peter Davies*)
Tremor of Intent
The Wanting Seed